James Davidson.
1855.

PARISH

AND

OTHER PENCILINGS.

BY KIRWAN,

AUTHOR OF

"LETTERS TO BISHOP HUGHES," "ROMANISM AT HOME," "MEN AND THINGS AS SEEN IN EUROPE," &c.

NEW YORK:

HARPER & BROTHERS, PUBLISHERS,

FRANKLIN SQUARE.

1854.

TO

THE REV. JOHN EDGAR, D.D.,

OF BELFAST, IRELAND,

THE LEARNED PROFESSOR, THE UNTIRING PHILANTHROPIST, THE FAITHFUL MINISTER, THE DEVOTED CHRISTIAN, THE TRUE MAN,

This Volume is Dedicated,

BY HIS FRIEND

THE AUTHOR.

PREFACE.

VERY early in my ministry I commenced noting peculiar providences, and making brief notes in reference to them. As I have had opportunity, these notes have been written out into brief articles, such as these which mostly compose the present volume. Some of them have been published under varying signatures, and have obtained through the religious press a wide circulation on both sides of the Atlantic. A few of them, reduced and compressed, have been published as tracts, and have in that form been widely scattered. I make this statement here, that none may be astonished at finding in these pages some articles they may have read with interest years ago, without knowing or caring who was their author.

Save the three articles on Dr. Duff and the Nuncio Bedini, none have been published over the *nom de plume* of the author; and these, with the article "Popery in the United States," have been inserted at the request of some friends, who deemed them worthy of preservation from the fate of most periodical essays —oblivion.

The subjects of some of these Pencilings will doubtless be recognized by persons residing in the places where the incidents narrated occurred. Making allowance for the difference caused by the different stand-points from which things are viewed, such will pronounce the narratives accurate. They are not fiction founded on fact. The same assurance is given as to those narratives whose subjects are not likely to be remembered. I have long ago rejected as greatly injurious, and as far-reaching in its evil tendencies, the principle of teaching religious truths under the garb of fiction. From much of the religious literature prepared for the young, the transition is much more easy and natural to the novel than to the Bible. Old people are often heard to complain of the slender and frail religious character of the rising generation. The cause may be traced to the trashy books prepared for the young, and for whose distribution the all-pervading agency of the Sabbath-school is not unfrequently invoked.

I am by no means indifferent to the reception which this volume may receive from the public. I invoke for it some of that kindness which has been shown to its predecessors; but my chief solicitude is, that it may be blessed of God to all who may favor it with a perusal. If it shall be blessed to the saving of one soul, I will thank God and take courage, and, perhaps, send forth another. Books are like sins—one is likely to bring another in its train.

CONTENTS.

PARISH PENCILINGS.

THE AURORA BOREALIS.

The sight described.

But few that saw it will ever forget the Aurora (or Northern Light) which occurred in the winter of 1836–7. It was pronounced, at the time, to be the most brilliant and general that had been seen by any living man. It was not confined, as it usually is, to the northern section of the heavens. The whole horizon was illumined by arches of fiery hue, from which columns and sheaves of light, of the most variegated and beautiful colors, shot up toward the zenith, forming there a fiery coronet of the most transcendent beauty. The agitation of these columns and sheaves was sometimes very great. Of a sudden these agitations would cease, and the light would die away, and the heavens would resume their wonted appearance; but in a moment these columns would shoot up again in increased size, and with greater splendor, giving an appearance of brilliancy and grandeur to the heavens which called forth the loud acclamations of the admiring beholders. For some weeks previous the earth had been covered with a deep snow, which a cold frost had made to sparkle with a peculiar brilliancy; and such was the effect upon it of the Aurora, that streets, fields, and houses looked as if they were covered with blood. This remarkable phenomenon only disappeared from the sky as the morning light began to dawn.

Not long afterward I observed, on Sabbath evening, and on the evening of the weekly service, in a corner of my lecture-room, a female who was a stranger to me, and, obviously, to the place. Her attention was marked; her attendance became regular. Weeks passed away without my knowing who she was. I received a request to visit a family where was a woman anxious about her soul. As I entered the door I was met by the stranger I had seen in the lecture-room. I was favorably impressed by her subdued and respectful manner, her great frankness and candor, and her deep solicitude to know the way to be saved. Taking my seat by her side, and after hearing her account of her feelings, I asked her if she understood the plan of salvation through Jesus Christ. Her reply was, "I am afraid I do not."

"Then, madam," said I, "will you permit me to explain it to you in a brief and simple manner?"

"That," said she, "is the very thing I want you to do."

"Well, then," said I, addressing her personally, and applying every word to herself, "you are a sinner in heart and in life. God is angry with you every day. Every sin you have ever committed deserves eternal banishment from God: so that you deserve to die as often as you have sinned. From the guilt and punishment of sin you can not relieve yourself—nor can man or angel relieve you—nor can baptism or the Lord's

Supper, or any other rite, relieve you. And such is the nature of your sin, and of the justice and government of God, that you can not be saved unless law and justice are satisfied for the many sins you have committed."

I stopped a moment to see the effect of all this upon her mind. Looking at me with a tearful eye, she replied in a subdued tone, "I feel all this in my soul. My fear of the anger of God which my sins have kindled is so great that I can not sleep or eat. My tears flow day and night."

But," said I, "there is a way of escape from the guilt and the punishment of sin. You are a sinner; and Jesus Christ has died for sinners. He bore the sins of all who ever have, or ever will believe upon him, in his own body on the tree. The law requires us to be righteous in order to enter heaven; and Christ Jesus is the end of the law for righteousness to every one that believes upon him. If you feel yourself to be a sinner, you have nothing to do but to believe in the Lord Jesus Christ in order to be saved. If you repent of sin, and believe in the Lord Jesus Christ—if you believe what Jesus teaches—if you do as he commands—if, now, without a moment's delay, you can trust your soul and its concerns in the hands of Jesus Christ, without waiting until you are either better or worse, he will certainly save you; for he says, "Come unto me, all ye that are weary and heavy laden, and I will give you rest."

With her bright and beaming eye fixed upon me, she drank in every word that I uttered; and when I concluded, she promptly replied, "This is just the way that suits my case." "Are you willing now," said I, "to believe in Christ, to cast yourself upon the merits of his atonement, to take him to be your Savior from all sin?" "Yes," said she, with the eagerness of a drowning man catching hold of the boat sent out to his rescue, "yes, I take him now to be my Savior; I cast myself now upon the merits of his atonement."

I prayed with her. When we arose from our knees her whole expression was changed, and a new song was put into her mouth. I felt there was a new trophy to redeeming grace and love before me.

I now felt greatly desirous to know something about her history, the leading incidents of which she gave me with great frankness. She was born and educated a Roman Catholic. Though well educated, she was, on the subject of religion, extremely ignorant. Although now in mid-life, and the mother of children, all the attention she ever gave to her soul was to go to mass and to confession; and even that she had given up for years, convinced of their utter worthlessness. And up to the evening of the Aurora Borealis, she never had a conviction of her sinfulness. With thousands of others, she gazed upon the brilliant heavens and the apparently crimsoned earth. The thought of the final conflagration, and of her utter unfitness to meet that dread scene, seized her mind, and she retired to her room deeply impressed with the greatness of God, and her own sinfulness and ingratitude. Then was made the first of those impressions which resulted in her conversion.

Her husband was a Frenchman, of Protestant parentage, but utterly regardless of religion. When he returned home on the evening of the day of my visit, she told him of my conversation with her, and its effects upon her mind and heart. She read to him from the Bible, and prayed with him. With his consent she erected the family altar. Her fidelity to him, and her deep anxiety for his salvation, created some restiveness, and he refused to hear her. In the deepest distress she sought my advice. I told her to increase her supplications for him in private, but to do nothing that would fret his mind, as that would be to defeat her great object. She retired resolved to follow my advice.

Some weeks had passed away without my knowing any thing of what was going on in this little family. On a Sabbath evening, after a day of peculiar solemnity in the house of the Lord, and when, with a dejected spirit, I was thinking that I had spent my strength for naught, she appeared in my study with her husband. She narrated her conversation and prayers with him, and he frankly confessed his opposition of heart to her change of mind, and especially to her conduct toward him in pressing religion upon him on all occasions. "But," said he, "her prayers and tears have broke my heart."

"I told John," said she, "that if you would tell him what you told me, he would love God too, and that he would feel better in his mind and heart. I have strove to tell him all, but he does not understand me well enough, and I wish you to tell him about Jesus Christ."

After hearing with intense interest their narratives as to each other's conduct, I spread out before John the plan of salvation, essentially as I had done a few weeks previous before his wife. When I got through, I asked him, "How does this plan appear to you?" His reply was, "It is the very one for me—I can now and cordially embrace it." I prayed with them, and when we rose from our knees John seemed a changed man. Before he left my study he felt that he could rejoice in Christ as his Savior.

Not long after, they professed their faith in Christ, and although for years beyond the bounds of my ministry, I believe they yet live to adorn that profession; and their conversion may be traced up, as a means under God, to the Aurora Borealis.

How plainly this narrative teaches the following truths:

The means of God for impressing the minds of sinners, and leading them to himself for pardon and salvation, are exhaustless.

A clear understanding of the plan of salvation through a Savior—of its freeness and fullness—of its sovereign efficacy when truly relied on, is the only sure way of securing peace to the anxious sinner.

How important that the believing wife should labor for the salvation of the unbelieving husband, and the believing husband for that of the unbelieving wife!

A word to the reader of this narrative. Are you a careless sinner? If the Aurora so impressed the mind of this woman, what will be your impressions when the elements shall melt with fervent heat—when the earth, with all that it contains, shall be consumed? Are you an anxious sinner? Then Jesus died for sinners; and he died for you, because you are a sinner. To be saved, you have only to believe upon him. Are you a Christian? Then rise from the perusal of this narrative with the resolution to labor for the conversion of some soul, as this woman labored for the conversion of her husband, and yours may not be a starless crown.

THE HAY-MOW.

My first settlement in the ministry was in a valley in one of the Middle States, beautiful beyond description. A broad and winding river enters it at the north, between two high, rocky peaks, which bear the evidence of being torn from each other's embrace by some dread concussion of nature; and, after a course of fifteen miles, takes its exit at the south, and through a gap probably made in the same way. On either side of this river the bottom-lands are exceedingly rich. As you leave the river, these lands gradually undulate, until, at the distance of about two miles, they rise into mountains on the east and west, which seem built of heaven to guard the quiet vale from all disturbing intrusions. As the traveler reaches the brow of the eastern mountain, a scene of surpassing loveliness spreads itself beneath him; and he feels that if peace has not utterly forsaken our world, its residence must be there. The valley seems as if expressly made for the home of the Indian; and for moons beyond the power of his arithmetic to calculate, the red man fished in that river, and planted his corn in that rich bottom, and sought his game upon the mountains. And before he could be compelled to yield it, he made the white man feel the power of his anger in many a dreadful surprise.

But sin, and in its very worst forms, found an entrance into this beautiful spot. Early in the history of the settlement, a church was collected there, which continued a feeble existence until 18—, when I became its pastor. Young, ardent, and without experience, I here commenced my ministry, in a community proverbial both for its intelligence and its disregard of religion; amid external opposition, and with a church small, and rent by internal discords. A more unpromising field none could desire.

I entered on my duties with zeal, and was diligent in their performance. I prepared my sermons with care, and thought them conclusive; but few heard them, and none seemed convinced by them. I felt deeply myself, but my hearers seemed unmoved. Months thus passed away without, to my knowledge, a religious impression being made on any mind; and, feeling that I labored in vain, and spent my strength for naught, I was about giving up in despair. My preaching seemed more to excite the opposition of the wicked than the prayers of the pious.

There was among my people a man in mid-life, a German by birth, and a remarkably simple-hearted, pure-minded Christian. Whoever was absent, he was always present at the place of prayer. One evening, early in December, as I was about retiring to rest, I heard a knock at my door, and my German friend was introduced, his countenance full of emotion. On taking his seat, his first words were these: "My dear pastor, I have come to tell you that the Lord is about to revive his work here." Surprised at his appearance and language, and at the lateness of his visit, I asked him, "Why do you think so?" He replied as follows: "About eight o'clock this evening, I went up to my hay-mow to give hay to my cattle, and while there the Spirit of God came upon me, and has kept me there praying until now. I feel that God is about to revive his work, and I could not go in to my family until I told you." The entire simplicity and earnestness of the good man convinced me that God had vouchsafed to visit his servant. After some conversation we parted, mutually agreeing to pray and labor for a revival of religion, and to engage as many as we could to do the same.

Every meeting for religious services was now to me one of intense interest. A few days convinced me that the spirit of prayer was on the increase. Meetings for prayer were numerously attended. The church on the Sabbath became more full and solemn; and a few weeks after that evening of wrestling with God on the hay-mow, found me in the midst of the first revival of my ministry, and one of the most precious I ever witnessed.

Permit me to narrate a few incidents which occurred during the progress of this revival, and which illustrate some great truths that should not be forgotten.

Among the first that expressed seriousness was a fashionable and well-educated young lady, belonging to one of our richest families. She was the pride of a mother whose ambition it was to have her shine in elegant society. Miss E—— expressed a hope in Christ. In a few days she was sent to spend the winter in one of our principal cities with some gay friends, who were directed to take her to all the fashionable amusements. She yielded to the temptation; and when she returned in the spring, seemed farther from the kingdom of heaven than ever. Another refreshing was soon enjoyed, when the former feelings of this young lady returned. She became hopefully pious, and in a few months the wife of a godly minister. And her large family, perhaps influenced by her example, followed her into the fold of Christ.

There was in the place a young man, a profane, but yet an industrious mechanic. Like Nicodemus, he came to me by night to know what he should do to be saved. His feelings seemed of the most pungent character, and his visits were often repeated. He thought he understood and could joyfully embrace the plan of salvation through Jesus Christ. Yielding to the influence of one wicked companion, in a few weeks he forsook the house of prayer and the people of God. As long as I knew him afterward, he was among the most obdurate men I ever knew. He ripened for ruin; and not long ago, with one stroke, as the woodman removes the saplings out of his way, God cut him down. It is a fearful thing to quench the Spirit!

Mr. C—— was a pleasant, moral, and interesting man. Under the prayers and conversations of a pious mother, he grew up a friend to the institutions of religion. His mind became deeply interested. But a more convenient season was always an excuse for the putting aside of present duty. In the midst of the revival, when some of the sturdy cedars of Lebanon were bowing, his aged mother, and with tears, besought him to make God his portion. "Mother," said he, "you are dependent upon me for a subsistence, and so are my motherless children. To provide for you all is my pleasure and my duty. I am now engaged in a very profitable work among the mountains, and when I have made enough to support you all comfortably, in connection with my own industry, I promise you I will attend to religion. But you must excuse me now." And with a solemn warning against the folly of such reasoning from the lips of his aged mother, he hastened to his business among the mountains. On the evening of the third day from his departure, he was brought back to that mother, and was laid at her feet a mutilated corpse. Before he could escape its track, a log of timber rolling down a steep precipice caught him, and, rolling over him, almost ground him to powder. And as we laid him down in the grave, I heard that mother exclaim, in the bitterness of her sorrow, "Would to God I had died for thee, my son, my son." Oh the folly of boasting of to-morrow, as we know not what a day may bring forth!

Some of our pious people undertook the circulation of religious tracts. The tract "The Way to be Saved" was selected for the purpose of placing in the hands of our people a plain and simple guide to to the Savior of sinners. One of these was placed in the shop of a mechanic who was noted for his profanity and vulgarity. Blotting out the word "saved" in the title of the tract, he wrote in its place "damned," so that the title, thus amended, read, "The Way to be Damned." Now tearing it nearly in two, he flung it into the street. It was soon picked up by a young woman, deeply serious, and who, although shocked by its title, carried it home. She read it with care; she pasted the torn leaves together, and read it again and again. She went as directed, and found peace and joy in believing. And in a conversation with her about her hope, she drew from her bosom this mutilated tract, saying, "This is the little book that told me the way to the cross." If yet alive, I have no doubt she preserves it among her choicest treasures. Thus it is that God often makes the wrath of man to praise him!

Many instances like these occurred during that revival, which the time would fail me to enumerate. But even these emphatically teach us,

1. That when faithfully and prayerfully discharging duty, ministers must not be unduly discouraged by unpropitious external circumstances. If they go forth weeping, bearing precious seed, they will return again with rejoicing, bringing their sheaves with them.

2. They teach us the power of prayer. It moves the hand that moves the world. That revival, with its consequent blessings, I have ever traced, under God, to that prayer on the hay-mow. The prayer that God inspires he will answer.

3. They teach us the awful guilt of parents who sacrifice the souls of their children at the shrines of worldly ambition. And, alas! how many such parents there are!

4. They utter warning notes in the ears of those who quench the strivings of the Spirit, or who post-

pone the duty of submission to God *now* to an uncertain future.

5. They teach us, that even pearls cast before swine may not be in vain. Through the wickedness of the wicked, God is ever accomplishing his purposes of love. How invincible the combined agencies of mercy, when even one mutilated tract becomes the instrument of life from the dead to a human soul!

Years have passed away since this revival occurred. Some of its subjects have already entered on its reward. That simple-hearted, pious German has gone up to his Savior. But the influences of that prayer on the hay-mow will live forever. Good men never die; they rest from their labors, but their works do follow them. May our churches never want members like him who wrestled and prevailed with God on the hay-mow.

THE TAP-ROOT.

On a bright and bracing afternoon, early in March, returning from a visit to an afflicted family, I met with one of my intelligent parishioners sitting on a fence. A gorgeous sunset was displaying its glories in the west, and my friend gave true indications that the day closing around us had not been spent in idleness. "What," said I, in a friendly tone of recognition, "are you doing here?" "I want," said he, "to transplant that pretty elm into my door-yard, and I have been laboring here for hours to dig it up, in vain. The tree, perhaps, is a little too old to be transplanted; but if removed early in the spring, and with a large root, trees frequently live, even beyond the age of this."

I crossed the fence to take a view of the tree. So finely formed was it, I wondered not at the desire to transplant it where its beauty might be observed and its shade be useful. I found it surrounded with a deep trench, and its lateral roots all cut; and feeling that a strong push would lay it on the earth, I gave it one. Not a twig nor a leaf moved the more on that account. I wondered, and turning to my friend, I asked, "Why is it so firm, when so many of its roots are cut, and when united to the earth by a stem so small?" "The tap-root," said he, "remains, and until that is cut it will remain firm." Hearing the phrase for the first time in my life, I asked, "What do you mean by the tap-root?" "Almost every tree," said he, "has its tap-root, which goes as straight down into the earth as the trunk goes into the air; and until that root is cut, the tree stands, and will grow. And if I should fill up this trench now, the tree would feel but little the cutting of all these lateral roots; they would soon grow out, and the tree would be as strong as ever."

We soon parted. I pursued my way home pondering these remarks. The tree was transplanted, and now stands, a noble and beautiful tree, just in the place selected for it. My friend has been transplanted to another world. Years have passed since the above conversation, but it has never been forgotten. It has suggested many truths to my mind, and it explains many things frequently occurring under our own observation, and which frequently cause doubt and hesitation. Some of these truths and things I will here state.

Are trees transplanted with difficulty after they have received a certain growth? This all admit. The rule is, to transplant them, whether fruit, forest, or ornamental, when young. Such is the law which rules in the kingdom of grace. "How can a man be born when he is old?" is a question of emphatic import to those who have grown up to mature years beyond the walls which inclose the Lord's vineyard.

Has almost every tree its tap-root? So every sinner has his besetting sin, which sustains him in his rebellion against God more than any other, and even when almost all others seem to be laid aside.

Are the lateral branches cut in vain until the tap-root is cut? Does the tree stand until the tap-root is severed? So, as far as their salvation is concerned, men are reformed in vain from immoral practices until the heart is converted. A depraved heart is the tap-root of that tree of evil which bears fruit unto death; and until that heart is taken away, the tree stands. Until this is effected, all reformation falls short of saving the soul.

Is the tree sustained by one root when all others are cut? Through that one root is it nourished into a permanent, if not a luxurious growth? So one sin unmortified, with its power over the soul unbroken, secures its final, its eternal loss.

How manifold are the illustrations of these truths in the Bible! Why did Balaam, who understood the will of God, and saw the visions of the Almighty, do as he did? Covetousness was his tap-root sin, and that was uncut. Why did Judas, after having preached the Gospel, and wrought miracles, and been numbered with the apostles, betray his master? The answer is the same. Why did Ananias and Sapphira, and Simon Magus, do as they did? The answer is the same. Why did the young man, who asked of Jesus what he should do to inherit eternal life, and whom Jesus loved, do as he did? In all these cases, covetousness was the tap-root sin, and that was uncut. O covetousness—often miscalled prudence and economy, but, by God, idolatry—how many souls hast thou destroyed, and art thou destroying!

But I have said that the above conversation with

my friend at the tree also explains many things frequently occurring, and which induce doubt and hesitation. Let me specify a few, by way of illustration.

Under the ministry of a faithful pastor sat an amiable man, with unfailing regularity, for years. All hoped he was a Christian. At each returning communion season it was expected that he would profess his faith in Christ; but he came not. None were more tender than he seemed; and his pastor supposed that he was kept from the communion of the saints only by that diffidence and distrust which are often the accompaniments of true piety. A truer explanation came at last. He loved strong drink, but took it only at night. The appetite grew until it vanquished shame, and he became a daily and open drunkard. He forsook the house and the ordinances of God. During the absence of his family at church on a certain Sabbath, he drank beyond measure—he fell into the fire—and when his family returned he was dead, and a portion of his body burned to a cinder! Why did not this man, in the days of his tears and tenderness, take Christ for his portion? The tap-root was not cut.

I knew a young man, who, although the child of praying parents, grew up an alien and outcast from the commonwealth of Israel. Grace is not hereditary; it is the gift of God. In a spiritual refreshing he was deeply convicted—he hoped he was converted. He sought admission to the Church; but fearing that all was not right, he was kindly requested to wait until the next communion season. In a few weeks afterward he sat at a gambling table until the stars were quenched in the light of the rising sun. And he continued until his death tenfold more the child of hell than he was before. The tap-root was not cut. Instances like these, without number, rise before me.

And the prevalence of some one sin — its reigning power over the soul—is the reason why every sinner that hears the Gospel does not believe it; or, that believes the Gospel, does not at once, by repentance toward God and faith in our Lord Jesus Christ, seek the salvation of his soul. And the remaining influence of a sin whose power has been broken, is the reason why any Christian fails in consecrating himself a living sacrifice to God.

Reader, are you a sinner convinced of the truth of the Gospel, without repentance, without faith in Christ? If so, how important to know the sin that holds you back from the work of your salvation. There is some one sin that does this more than any other, perhaps more than all others. What is it?

A careful pondering of these questions may lead you to its discovery. What are the objects that most delight you? What are the gratifications on which you bestow most time? thoughts as to what most intrude themselves when alone? The last thing which the sailor throws overboard, in his efforts to save his sinking vessel, is that which he deems most precious; what is the sin you are most anxious to retain? When you think of being a Christian, what is the sin, the pursuit, the habit, that you feel in prospect would give you the most pain to abandon? These questions point to your besetting sin—your tap-root sin. Unless cut, you are lost.

But if old trees can not be transplanted, may not old sinners be converted? Yes, they may. As to aged sinners, the difficulty lies in the nature of man, and of sin, and of evil habits, and not in the grace of God. Grace is all-conquering when God sees fit to apply it. Reader, are you an aged sinner? I have seen the man, fourscore and two years old, who bled in the battles of the Revolution—who learned its worst vices, and continued in their practice until the age stated, hopefully converted. I have seen him brought, trembling with palsy, in his arm-chair, to God's house, and there joining himself to the people of God; and having commemorated the love of Christ, lifting up his withered hands to heaven in thanksgiving for the mercies vouchsafed. And his subsequent life and triumphant death testified that the work was of God. But in my experience, this stands out a solitary case, to check presumption on the one hand, and despair on the other.

Reader, as you lay down this volume, after reading this article, take these thoughts for your meditation:

1. You have a besetting sin, stronger in its bad influence over you than any other.

2. It is of the highest importance to you to know what it is. Resolve to know it.

3. Reformation is not conversion. The tree stands when all its lateral roots are cut.

4. Unless by the grace of God your heart is changed, all is vain. The tree of evil, whose fruit is death, remains, because the tap-root is not cut.

5. However aged or wicked, there is grace and power to meet your case. Seek them without delay, and aright, and they are yours.

THE BIRD IN THE CHURCH.

The town of E—— is embowered in trees. Its ancient and spacious church, with its chiming clock, and towering steeple of beautiful proportions, although in the centre of the town, is yet in the centre of forest trees, which nearly conceal it from view; and, what is more, it is the centre and home of the affections of a people whose ancestors for nearly two hundred years have there worshiped God in spirit and in truth.

And that ancient church is associated with many and wonderful displays of sovereign grace. It has been the birth-place of souls, the house of God, and the gate of heaven to multitudes. Under its ample roof thousands have consecrated themselves to God, and amid the ordinances there dispensed, have ripened for glory.

In the year 18—, the people of E—— were favored with, perhaps, the most signal work of grace they ever enjoyed. The whole community was moved to its deep foundations, and persons of all ages and classes were in the pursuit of salvation as the great end of their being. Many, the blessed fruits of that revival, continue until the present day.

On a Sabbath of that year of unusual brilliancy, in the late spring, that church was crowded with multitudes anxious about their souls, and hanging upon the lips of their beloved pastor, who, with earnestness and tears, was expounding to them the way of reconciliation with God. Every thing in the external world—the balmy and reviving breezes—the new and beautiful dress which fields and forests were putting on—the trees budding, or in blossom—the blossoms setting in fruit, were in sympathy with the feelings of this worshiping people, and were but emblems of the spiritual transformations which were in progress among them.

On this Sabbath the doors of the church were open, and the windows were all closed. During the progress of the service, a bird entered by the door, and flew up to the vaulted roof, and, alarmed by the voices which it heard, gave every evidence of anxiety to make its escape. There sat in one of the pews a female under deep conviction for sin, and who, for months, had been seeking, without finding, peace for her soul. Her eye soon lit upon the fluttering bird, and followed him from window to window, in his vain efforts to escape. It sought an exit at every window, and almost at every pane of glass; and as it fluttered from one window to another, this female would say in her heart, "O foolish bird, why strive to get out there? is not the door wide open?" It would now rise to the ceiling—now renew its vain attempts at the windows; this female repeating to herself, "O foolish bird, why strive to get out there? is not the door wide open?" And when its wings were weary, and when all hope of escape seemed to be abandoned, and, as if unable to sustain itself longer, it lowered itself into the body of the church, caught a view of the door, and was out in a moment, singing a song of triumph over its release, amid the branches of the trees.

When the bird was gone, the thoughts of this female reverted to her own state and doings. The voice of the preacher was unheard amid the conflicts of her own thoughts. "I have been acting," said she, "like that foolish bird. I have been seeking peace in ways in which it is not to be found, and to go out from the bondage of sin through doors that are closed against me. Christ is the door; through him there is escape from the dominion of sin. I have acted like that foolish bird long enough. What the door was to it, Christ is to me. As it escaped through the door, so may I through Christ." And she found peace in believing. And almost as soon as the bird commenced its melody in the trees, rejoicing over its escape, she commenced making melody in her heart unto the Lord.

Years passed away, and her peace flowed like a river whose gentle stream is never excited into a ruffle. Subsequently she had her periods of occasional depression, but without ever forgetting that Christ is the door. Threescore years and ten passed away, and amid the infirmities of age Christ was yet precious as the door. She has recently put off her earthly tabernacle; and from the day that she saw that bird in the church, until the day that she passed in, through Christ the door, amid the spirits of the just made perfect, she never gave ground for a reasonable doubt that Christ was in her the hope of glory.

How infinitely diversified are the ways and instrumentalities by which sinners are led to be reconciled to God! "The wind bloweth where it listeth, and thou hearest the sound thereof, but canst not tell whence it cometh or whither it goeth; so is every one that is born of the Spirit."

And how truthful the application of the folly of that bird, by that female, to her own case! And is not its folly the folly of every sinner? The first right feeling of a sinner returning from the error of his ways is a sense of his deep sinfulness in the sight of God. If this feeling is never felt, then, in ordinary cases, there is no return to God—we must die aliens to God, and continue outcasts from the light of the universe forever. But when the Spirit convinces and convicts of sin, how often is deliverance sought from it in the ways that the bird vainly sought to escape from the church! The sinner flees to every thing that gives hope of deliverance but to the right thing. The Bible is read—prayer is made—sin is abstained from—the worship of God is frequented—the advice of Christian people is sought; but there is no escape from the dominion of sin—none from a sense of guilt, nor from the fear which it inspires. All these are but as the windows to the bird, which gave it hope that it might escape through them because they admitted the light. When it failed at one it flew to another; each window, in its turn, excited hope, and in every case the hope excited was dashed by the trial to escape. When all is done, the weight of sin yet hangs upon the soul. And the reason is, there is yet no recourse to the remedy for sin, to the door of escape from its power and guilt. CHRIST is that remedy. Christ is that door. And so prone are men to do something to save themselves, that until all they can do is tried in vain, they will not look unto "the Lamb of God, that taketh away the sin of the world."

The great central truths of Christianity, so far as men are concerned, are these: we are sinners; Christ Jesus has died to atone to law and justice for the sins of sinners, and whosoever believes on the Lord Jesus Christ shall be saved. Reader, do you hope you are a Christian? If so, you know all this by experience. Never cease telling these truths to all men as you have opportunity. Are you a sinner convicted of your sin, and seeking deliverance from it? Then imitate not the bird which sought an exit through the closed windows, to the forgetfulness of the open door. Waste not your time, and spend not your strength for naught in seeking relief at sources that never can yield it. Go at once to Christ; ponder this one truth until it is written in letters of living light upon your soul, "He that believeth on the Lord Jesus Christ shall be saved." Faith in Jesus Christ will save you; nothing else can.

THE FEARFUL FUNERAL.

It was on the morning of a cold, chilly day in the month of April that I was thus interrupted in my studies by one of my children: "Pa, there is a queer-looking man in the parlor who wants to see you." On entering the room, my eye lit upon a man who was queer-looking indeed, because his face, dress, and whole appearance proclaimed him a drunkard. He rose on my entering the room, and, with that constrained and awkward politeness, amounting to obsequiousness, which the half-intoxicated often assume, he thus addressed me:

"I come, sir, to ask you to attend a funeral this afternoon."

"Who," said I, "is dead?"

"A friend of mine," he replied, "by the name of S——; and as he has no particular friends here, I thought I would come and ask you."

"Where did he live?" I again asked.

"Why," said he, "he lived no place in particular, except at the grocery of Mr. ———." This Mr. ——— was the keeper of a groggery of the very lowest character, where blacks and whites freely mingled in their revels, and which had often been presented as a nuisance.

I again asked, "Of what disease did he die?"

"Why," said he, dropping his countenance, and lowering his voice almost to a whisper, "I hardly know; but, between you and I, he was a pretty hard drinker."

After a few more inquiries, to which I received answers in keeping with those given above, I dismissed him, promising to attend the funeral at five o'clock.

At the hour appointed, I went to the house of death. There were ten or twelve men present, and, with two exceptions, they were all drunkards. I went up to the coarse pine coffin, and gazed upon a corpse, not pale and haggard, but bloated, and almost as black as the raven's wing. There were two brothers present, both inebriates, and as unfeeling as if the body of a beast lay dead before them. From the undertaker I gained the following narrative as to the deceased:

"He was the son of respectable but irreligious parents, who, instead of spending the Sabbath in the house of God, either spent it in idleness or in doing their own work." When desecrated, the Sabbath is usually a day of fearful temptation. Sabbath sins make deep impressions on the soul. "While yet young, he became a Sabbath vagrant, joined profane companions, acquired the habit of drinking, and so rapidly grew the love of drink into a ruling passion, that at mature years he was a confirmed drunkard. His parents died, and the portion of property that fell to his lot was squandered. And for years," said my informant, "he has been drunk every day."

"But how," I asked, "did he get the money to pay for the liquor?"

"He has been employed," he replied, "by Mr. ——— to shoot squirrels in the woods, and to catch water-rats in the marshes; and for the skins of these he has been paid in whiskey. Nobody would see him starve, and he usually slept in a garret over the groggery. Yesterday he was taken sick, very sick, in the grocery; Mr. ———, instead of giving him a bed, turned him out of the house. He was then in a dying state, and, at a short distance from the house, fell in the street. He was taken into a negro hut and laid on the floor, where he died in less than an hour. The negroes were very ignorant and superstitious, and were afraid to have the corpse in their house. It was carried to a barn. This poor but pious family, hearing the circumstances, took the corpse to their house, and have made these preparations for its burial."

I read a portion of the Scriptures, and for a few moments discoursed to them on the effects of sin; I dwelt on the hardening and fearful effects of intemperance. But there was no feeling. I prayed with them, but there was no reverence. They all gazed with a vacant stare, as if their minds had evaporated, and as if the fiery liquid had burned out their consciences. They were obviously past feeling. The coffin was closed and placed in the hearse. We proceeded with slow and solemn pace to the house appointed for all the living; and a feeling of shame came over me as I passed along the street, to be followed by half a dozen pair of inveterate topers. The coffin was placed upon the bier, and was carried by four drunkards, who were actually reeling under their load, to a secluded spot in the grave-yard, where, without a tear being shed, without a sigh being uttered, it was covered up under the cold clods of the valley; and the two brothers went back to the house of death, the grog-shop, to drink, and to die a similar death, and to go early down to the same ignoble grave. The others, after lingering for a few moments, as if arrested by the thought that the grave would be soon their house, followed. I stood for a short time over the grave after all had retired, pondering the deeply-impressive scenes through which I had so rapidly passed. "And is this," said I to myself, "the grave of the drunkard?" And the prayer, almost unconsciously, rose from my heart to heaven, "O God, save my children's children to their latest generation from making such a contribution as this to the congregation of the dead."

As I retired from the grave-yard, the following lessons, suggested and illustrated by this narrative, were deeply impressed on my mind:

1. How great is the responsibility of parents! With what moral certainty they form the character of their children after the model of their own! Careless and irreligious themselves, their children copy their example; but, because destitute of their firmness of character, they yield to every temptation, until they can commit sin with greediness. Were the parents of this young man, who was laid down in a drunkard's grave, on which no tear of sorrow has ever fallen, truly and consistently pious, how different might have been his life and his death! How many parents lay the foun-

dation for the temporal and eternal ruin of their children!

2. How sad the effects which usually follow the habitual violation of the Sabbath! All need the checks and the restraints which the due observance of the Sabbath places upon our depravity. The habitual violators of the Sabbath are usually those hardened in the ways of sin; and to become the associates of such is to insure the end of the proverb, "The companion of fools shall be destroyed." Had this young man been brought up to "remember the Sabbath day," he might have been saved to the cause of virtue and usefulness, and from an early, ignoble, and unknown grave. The due observance of the Sabbath is alike necessary to the attainment of temporal and spiritual good.

3. How selfish and hard the hearts of those who live by rum! It is a base business to sell it by small quantities for the sake of making a living. It is in opposition to divine, and usually to human law. And so plainly is it under the ban of the world's reprobation, that but few, save "the hardened wicked," engage in it. And if a man of kind and generous nature engages in it, his heart soon becomes a heart of steel. Mr. ———, the keeper of the grocery, was naturally a kind man; he became a seller of liquor, against law, by the small measure. He kept and fed poor S—— as long as he was able to shoot squirrels or rats. Many is the day he spent in the salt marshes to earn his whiskey. And when his poor frame gave way under the vile work, the man who did so much to degrade him turned him out to die in the street. There is not

a class of men upon earth who deserve so little at the hands of their fellow-men as do these retailers of liquid death by the gill!

4. How degrading is the vice of intemperance! It ruins soul, body, and character. And by elevating a mean appetite above reason, and conscience, and judgment, it degrades man to the level of the brute. Here was a young man, of respectable parentage, who, by taking glass after glass, became a drunkard. Habitual intemperance unfitted him for any business; he became the tenant of a low grocery, the fumes from which, of a winter evening, were sickening; he became the slave of a low grocer—for to earn a glass of whiskey, he would spend the day and sometimes the night in the salt marshes catching rats. When no longer able to earn his glass, he was turned out to die. After he breathed his last in a negro hut, his corpse was taken to a barn; by the charity of the pious alone was his dead body saved from exposure, and by the hands of drunkards he was carried to an ignoble grave, unwept and unregretted. And all this is only the degradation which it brings on the body! It is an immutable law of Jehovah that no drunkard shall ever inherit the kingdom of God.

Drunkenness is thus characterized by Watson, an old Puritan divine: "There is no sin which doth more efface God's image than drunkenness. It disguiseth a person and doth even unman him. Drunkenness makes him have the throat of a fish, the belly of a swine, and the head of an ass. Drunkenness is the shame of nature, the extinguisher of reason, the shipwreck of chastity, and the murder of conscience. Drunkenness is hurtful to the body—the cup kills more than the cannon. It causeth dropsies, catarrhs, apoplexies; it fills the eyes with fire, and the legs with water, and turns the body into a hospital. But the greatest hurt it doth is to the soul; excess of wine breeds the worm of conscience. The drunkard is seldom reclaimed by repentance, and the ground of it is partly because, by this sin, the senses are so enchanted, the reason so impaired, and lust so inflamed; and partly it is judicial, the drunkard being so besotted by his sin, God saith of him, as of Ephraim, he is joined to his cups, let him alone; let him drown himself in liquor until he scorch himself in fire."

O reader, beware of drunkenness; it is a degrading, damning sin. If you have already so far yielded to temptation as to have acquired a relish for it, resolve now never to taste again the fiery liquid. Remember the fearful funeral of the drunkard.

THE BRILLIANT STAR.

Who, in our northern latitudes, has not often gazed with wonder and admiration upon the sky, when a clear, cold wintry night adds new beauty to its magnificent scenery? When the atmosphere is cloudless, and the cold is severe, as if to compensate for the desolation that reigns on the earth, the heavens put on new beauty, and the moon and the stars shine with unwonted and sparkling brilliancy; and stupid must be the mind, and senseless the soul, that, canopied by such a wintry sky, does not ponder, wonder, and adore. We can readily believe that it was while gazing upon such a sky David was inspired to write the psalm in which he thus expresses the emotions that well up within him: "When I consider thy heavens, the work of thy fingers, the moon and the stars which thou hast ordained, what is man, that thou art mindful of him, and the son of man, that thou visitest him?" He is overpowered by the scenes of grandeur which surround him, and wonders that he is not forgotten amid the cares which an empire so vast devolves upon the High and lofty One.

It was on such a wintry night that the following incident occurred: The sky was cloudless, the cold was intense, the very air seemed frozen into stillness; the earth was covered with a deep snow, which added at once to the brilliancy and dreariness of the scenery. There sat by a cheerful fire, in one of our rural villages, a young lady of fine intellect, and highly cultivated. Although religiously educated, and often deeply solicitous about her salvation, she was, up to this time, a stranger to the grace of God, and was on this evening more than usually careless. Attracted by some noise in the street, she went to the window. Her attention was immediately arrested by the remarkable beauty of the heavens, and by the sparkling of the stars. She stood gazing on the splendid panorama in mute admiration. One star of remarkable brilliancy attracted her eye. The more she gazed on it the more she admired it, and as she gazed, it seemed to increase in size and brilliancy, until it filled the field of vision —until the lesser lamps which hung around it went out in the effulgence of its light. This glowing, brilliant, admired star at once suggested the "Star of Bethlehem;" and, almost unconscious to herself, she commenced humming the well-known lines of Kirke White:

"When marshalled on the nightly plain,
The glittering host bestud the sky,
One star alone of all the train
Can fix the sinner's wandering eye."

Soon the star in the sky was forgotten amid the thoughts concerning Christ that rushed in upon her. The Divine Spirit, at times, performs its peculiar work with great rapidity. Her mind wandered from the star in the sky to the "Star of Bethlehem," then to Jesus Christ. The question rapidly arose, Why did

Christ come in the flesh? why did he die? Her intelligent mind and her right education promptly suggested the true answer, He came to save sinners, and he died the just for the unjust. With the rapidity of a mind waked up by the Spirit to a due sense of the guilt and danger of an unconverted soul, she ran to the conclusion, "Then I am a sinner, and I need a Savior." And with these two thoughts written upon her soul as with the point of a diamond, she retired from the window to her chair by the fire, the arrows of conscience piercing her through and through. Whatever was the character of her previous convictions, these were obviously the work of the Spirit. She sought mercy in that way in which the Lord has never failed to grant it — in the way of repentance toward God, and faith in the Lord Jesus Christ. The light of the "Star of Bethlehem" illumined her soul. She connected herself with the Church of Christ, and, amid scenes of activity, and usefulness, and happiness, she often sang as to that star,

"It was my guide, my light, my all,
It bade my dark forebodings cease;
And through the storm and danger's thrall
It led me to the port of peace."

This incident teaches many lessons of great practical importance, to a few of which we ask the serious attention of the reader.

1. It teaches us how various are the means by which God accomplishes his own purposes of grace. While the preaching of the Gospel is the great means for leading sinners to a Savior, it is not the only means.

A Jewish maid, and a slave in the family of Naaman, was the cause of his washing in the Jordan, and of his cure from the disease of leprosy, and, as is believed, of his conversion; the Church is indebted for Samuel to the prayers of his mother; Paul was arrested by a voice from heaven; Luther was converted by the reading of the Bible; Newton, during a storm at sea; multitudes by the reading of a book or a tract; and this young woman by the brilliant shining of a star on a wintry night. If "the invisible things of him from the creation of the world are clearly seen, being understood by the things that are made, even his eternal power and godhead," may he not use all the things which he has made as agents to direct men unto the Lamb of God that taketh away the sin of the world? And we believe that a true history of the conversion of men would show that all the things which God has made have been made subservient to the accomplishment of his purposes of mercy and grace. None should therefore be anxious as to the agency employed; the great question is as to the result, Have I been led to Christ?

2. It teaches us the need of the Spirit to render means effectual to salvation. Without it no means can arrest the wandering mind or change the heart; with it, the most feeble means are effectual to produce these results. This all are made to feel. The most faithful and powerful preaching is in vain without the Spirit; without it, in the use of means, we are as one that beateth the air; with it, the most feeble means are powerful to the conversion of the most hardened

and hopeless. This young female had heard many a sermon — was often deeply impressed; of the truth of religion she was fully convinced. And although brought up amid the very sunlight of truth, never was she led to believe with the heart unto salvation until her attention was arrested by the bright shining of that star on a wintry night. Surely Paul may plant, and Apollos may water, but it is God alone that can give the increase. And as it is the Spirit that takes of the things of Christ, and that shows them unto us, the cry of the Church, and of every individual to whom the news of this salvation is sent, should be for the Spirit. Then the glorious sun, the silvery moon, the twinkling star, the little tract, the larger volume, the stately tome, will all be found co-working with the Bible and the preaching of the Gospel to direct sinners unto the Lamb of God that taketh away the sins of the world. Then truths are taught by stones, sermons are preached by brooks, every star in the sky is associated with the Star of Bethlehem, and God is seen every where.

3. It teaches us how inexcusable are sinners for not believing in Christ. If the law and the prophets all point to his coming, the law and the prophets, and the apostles and evangelists, all teach us that it is only through faith in him we can be saved. Conscience unites with revelation in teaching us that we are sinners. And the clearest deductions of our minds unite with conscience and revelation in teaching us that he that believeth in the Son hath life, and he that believeth not in the Son shall not see life, but the wrath of God abideth on him. And to the Savior of sinners

God is directing us by all the things which he has made—by all the occurring providences around us—by all the means of grace which he has appointed. And if the light of that star brilliantly shining in a wintry sky led that careless mind to the Star of Bethlehem—thence to the coming and to the cross of Christ—thence to her own sinfulness and to her need of a Savior—thence to the exercise of faith in him, what can excuse your unbelief when truth and duty stand revealed before you in the meridian light of heaven—when the cross of Christ rises before you as the only hope of the sinful—when the Spirit and the bride are uniting their voices with those of the Bible, and of the ministry, and of your mind, and of your conscience, entreating, imploring you to believe in the Lord Jesus Christ, that you may be saved?

THE ONE TALENT SANCTIFIED.

Among individuals religiously educated, and brought into the Church under the ordinary means of grace, it is at times difficult to discriminate between what is the result of education and habit, and what of the teachings and influence of the Divine Spirit. The line which separates these it is difficult, perhaps impossible, clearly to draw. A religious education is a powerful means of grace; and so gently and quietly do the rain and dew of the Spirit descend upon the seed thus sown in the youthful mind, that oftentimes the result, which is love to God, would seem to be a fruit, not of spiritual agency, but of natural growth; and oftentimes, on self-examination, the most intelligently pious find themselves in difficulty and in darkness because of their inability to distinguish between the influence of education, theory, and custom, and the work of the Spirit on their hearts and lives. This truth, every where felt in the experience of the pious, often gave rise to the wish that I might become acquainted with somebody who, on the subject of religion, knew nothing but what was taught by the Spirit. I supposed there would be a freshness and a simplicity about the exercises of such that would place them in broad contrast with those which are more or less fashioned by our theoretic views of divine truth, and by the habits and forms into which we are educated. And of such an individual I became, on my second settlement, the pastor.

On Sabbath morning, as I was retiring from the church, after preaching my first sermon to my new charge, I was arrested by a man in the belfry in a way peculiar and striking. His garb was plain—his form of the middle size—his countenance had a vague, but yet a pleased expression. Without waiting for an introduction, he came forward and earnestly extended his hand to grasp mine. The pressure was painfully cordial; and while one hand pressed mine, and the other his own bosom, he said, "I thank you for that sermon; it has done my soul good." His voice was indistinct and husky, and his appearance not prepossessing; but there was a heartfelt cordiality in his greeting which impressed me with his thorough sincerity. On the next Sabbath, and on the next, he met and greeted me in the same way. As he had reached mid-life, I marked him as a peculiar character.

I soon visited the Sabbath-school; and the very first person that arrested my attention was this man, sitting in one of the classes surrounded by young boys, and reciting with them his lesson. My curiosity being excited, I went and stood by his class, and found him spelling his way through a verse of one of the Gospels, and obviously without understanding the sentiment which it taught. On inquiry, I learned that he was the son of Christian parents; that his mother, who was a woman of marked piety, had been deceased for years; and that, because of the great feebleness of his intellect, he could never be taught to read. As the name of the Savior was constantly on his lips, as his piety seemed to be of the most ardent character, my curiosity was greatly quickened to learn the details of his religious history, which is briefly as follows:

As his mental debility early developed itself, his pious mother became the more solicitous that he should be taught of the Spirit of God. Daily did she pray with him; and, selecting the simplest truths of the Gospel, daily did she seek to impress them on his mind. But if his mind was feeble in sense, his heart was strong in depravity, and these means were ineffectual. After he reached mature years, there occurred a gentle refreshing of the Spirit. A meeting for conference with the serious and inquiring was appointed, and he was among those who attended. From week to week his seat was never vacant. When candidates for the communion of the Church were invited to meet with the session, he was among those that attended. When asked if he hoped he was a Christian, his emphatic reply was, "I hope I am." About the doctrines of the Church he knew absolutely nothing, and when questioned in reference to them, he made no reply. He could give no reason for the hope which was in him. When asked why he hoped he was a Christian, laying his hands on his heart, he answered, "I feel that I am here." With some fears, he was admitted to the Lord's Supper, and the whole of his subequent life demonstrated that he was born from above.

In the year that he made a profession of religion his mother died. Feeble as was his mind, the impressions which she made upon it were never erased. His very highest conception of heaven was that it was the place where his mother went to see Jesus, and his highest ecstacy was induced by the thought that when he died he would go to heaven to see Jesus and his own dear mother.

There was but one thought which seemed to enter his soul, and that entirely occupied it. This was constantly obvious. Preach on what subject I might, nothing was understood, nothing felt, unless it was the love of Christ. For years, rarely a Sabbath passed away without his greeting me in the belfry; but nothing was said about the sermons unless they dwelt upon the love of Christ. Then his usual expression was, "That sermon is good to my soul; it told me about the love of Christ."

He frequented prayer-meetings sustained by the young people and for their mutual benefit. One of his weaknesses was to make exhortations in these meetings, and until they became an annoyance. But he never succeeded in getting beyond one idea; and upon that—"the love of Christ, the love of Christ"—he would ring changes for fifteen minutes together. That one idea occupied and filled his whole soul. It was the one constant theme of his conversation every where. The only hymn that ever seemed to have impressed him, or whose singing he ever seemed to enjoy, was that called "Loving Kindness." However dull and uninterested he seemed to be in a prayer-meeting, the moment the first notes of the hymn

"Awake, my soul, to joyful lays,
And sing thy great Redeemer's praise,"

fell upon his ear, his countenance brightened up, and his whole soul was in sympathy with the song of praise. And when in a social meeting which did not greatly interest him, his peculiar voice was often heard saying, "Sing Loving Kindness."

His zeal, though not always according to knowledge, was of the purest character, and knew no relaxation. Was any person sick in his neighborhood? He was among the first to find it out and to visit the sick-bed. And feeble as was his comprehension of truth, and broken and repetitious as were his prayers, I have often heard the sick speak of the comforts which they received from his visits. He often preceded the minister and the elder—often conveyed to them the information of sickness and affliction, and solicited their attention; and often prayed and exhorted where their services might not be kindly received. The perfect confidence entertained by all in his sincerity induced them to forget his extreme feebleness, to overlook what would be regarded as intrusion in others, and to put the best possible construction on all that he did. I heard a profane scoffer say, after recovering from a sick-bed on which he had been often visited by this man, "Well, if there is a Christian upon earth, it is Uncle Nehemiah." More than once, when his minister was sick and in affliction, did he come and ask the privilege of praying with him and his family. Such was his life for years together.

And in full keeping with his life was his death.

During the protracted sickness which brought his days to their close, I frequently visited him. There was an unshaken confidence in Christ—a cloudless enjoyment of the light of his countenance; the love of Christ was his constant theme. The very last words that he ever uttered in my hearing were about going to heaven to see Jesus Christ and his dear mother.

There are a few truths which this narrative of the life and death of "Uncle Nehemiah," as he was familiarly called, forcibly teach and illustrate.

1. It teaches us how deep and durable are the impressions which may be made on the minds of her children by a pious mother. Here was a mind, because of its feebleness, difficult of impression; yet a pious mother so impressed it, so engraved her own image upon it, as that nothing could erase her impressions or image. How deeply must it have been impressed with a sense of her piety, when its highest idea of heaven was that it was the home of Jesus and his mother! What might the sons of the Church be, if all their mothers were like the mother of Nehemiah!

2. It illustrates the truth of the great doctrine of regeneration. This consists, not in submission to the ordinances and forms of religion, but in being created anew in Christ Jesus. In his youth, Nehemiah was wayward, and, like persons of mental feebleness generally, greatly under the influence of passion. Submission to ordinances and forms could not correct this; the formal Jew, the Papist, the Mohammedan, can go out from their most solemn ritual observances as wicked and as turbulent as ever. Nothing but a

change at the great spring of life can permanently change the life. There was no intellectual power here to moralize—no judgment to strengthen—no reason to wake up to its duty — no capacity to instruct. And yet there is a great, obvious, and permanent change. How account for it? In no way save on the ground of a change of heart by the power of the Holy Ghost.

3. It also illustrates what is the great saving truth of tho Gospel. It is a simple view of Christ as the Savior of sinners, and a simple resting upon him as our Savior. Other truths are important—they are important to a well-balanced faith and life, but the great, essential truth is faith in Christ. "He that believeth in the Lord Jesus Christ shall be saved." This is so plain, that a wayfaring man, though a fool, need not err respecting it. When this faith is wrought in us by the Holy Ghost, then, whether we possess the expansive intellect of Paul, or the feeble one of Nehemiah, Christ is the polar star of the soul.

Oh, if all the intellectual endowments of the professors of the religion of Christ were consecrated to his service, as was the one talent of this feeble child of heaven, how soon would the wilderness and solitary portions of earth rejoice, and the desert blossom as the rose! How hath God chosen the foolish things of the world to confound the mighty!

THE DANGER OF DELAY.

"I hope my time will come yet."

A FEW years ago, many of the veterans of the war of the Revolution were found scattered over the Eastern, Middle, and Southern States, the remnants of that noble generation who plighted their lives, property, and sacred honor to secure the liberty of our country. Among these were men who went from their knees to the battle strife, and who returned from the field of their victory or defeat to their closets, to lay down their palms and laurels before God, or most humbly to deplore the sins which caused them to flee before the enemy, and to implore the interposition of Almighty power in the next conflict to which they should be called. Among them, also, were men who carried with them through all their subsequent life the vices acquired in the camp, and that indifference to religion, which, alas! so frequently accompanies the profession of arms. The heart in which those stern and tumultuous passions reside which fit man for a brave soldier, and which are nurtured into a vigorous growth by actual and hard service, is usually a heart difficult to be impressed with the great truths of the Gospel.

There was in my congregation, when I became its pastor, one of these noble men, far advanced in life, in whom I became quite interested. When I first saw him he had passed his fourscore years, and, although exceedingly feeble, his large frame and his flashing eye bore abundant testimony to what he once was. Although in private life a most amiable and inoffensive man, he indulged too freely in strong drink, and was utterly careless as to his future state. In my occasional interviews with him, I found him always ready to converse on topics pertaining to the war of our Independence, but upon religious topics he was utterly silent, save in assenting or dissenting by a "yes" or "no" to my questions.

Hearing that he was quite sick, and rapidly approaching the close of his long life, I hastened to see him. It was on a cold day in early winter. I found him bolstered up in a large armed-chair, and covered with warm clothing, and sitting in front of a fire toward which he was a little inclined, sustaining himself with a staff which he grasped with his tremulous hands. A more striking illustration of the utter feebleness to which age may reduce the strongest frame I never saw. The suns of almost ninety years had now rolled over him; and although utterly helpless as to his body, his mind was clear and collected. I sat by his side, and as kindly and tenderly, but yet as pointedly as I could, I spoke to him of sin, and of death, and of judgment, and of salvation through faith in the finished work of Jesus Christ. He assented to all I said. I told him that the sands in his glass were almost run—that the grave must soon be made his house—and I sought to impress upon him the infinite need there was of employing the last and rapidly waning hour of life in securing the salvation of his soul. I told him of Manasseh, who in old age lifted up his bloody hands for mercy to heaven, and found it. I told him of the dying thief, who, in the agonies of death, implored mercy from a Savior, and received it. Hoping from his appearance that I had excited a little emotion, I asked him directly, Do you feel that you are a sinner? "O yes," he replied. "Do you think that you can go to heaven without faith in Jesus Christ?" I again asked him. He hesitated a moment, but emphatically replied "No." Feeling that I had now a ground upon which I could strongly press home immediate duty, I again asked him, "Why not commit your sinful soul this moment into the hands of Jesus Christ, who says to you as well as to all men, 'Him that cometh unto me I will in no wise cast out?'"

He hesitated for a few moments. I resolved not to break the silence. I watched every movement of his countenance to see if I could read the emotions of his soul. Feeling that I was waiting for a reply to my last question, he made a slight effort to rise from his inclined position, and finally said, in a low and tremulous voice, "I hope my time will come yet!" Never did I hear a sentence fall from human lips which more deeply affected me, or which has been more constantly before my mind. It swept from me at once the fond hopes I was beginning to indulge that he yet might be saved—it seemed to ring the very death-knell of his soul. Going on to ninety years—unable to get up or lie down of himself—with his grave just before him—confessing his belief in all the great truths of the Gospel, and yet, when pressed to lay hold on Christ as an all-sufficient Savior, turning away from eternal life, saying, "I hope my time will come yet!" The delusion seemed awful!

But that time never came. He lingered on a few weeks. One spring of life failed after another. Soon all access to his mind was closed; and after lingering in perfect unconsciousness of all that was passing around him for a few days, his immortal spirit went up to the judgment. His hope was as the spider's web. His time never came.

The incident teaches many important lessons worthy the serious consideration of every thinking man.

1. It teaches us the extent to which this fallacious hope prevails. We find it on the lips of youth, who, although persuaded of the truth of religion, will not surrender the pursuit of unsatisfying pleasure to embrace Christ. It is on the tongue of those in mid-life, who are so much concerned in the things of a day as to have no time for the things of eternity. And we find it on the faltering tongue of old age, when the candle of life, burned down to the socket, is emitting its last lurid rays. Although the excuse of a heart in love with sin and averse to God, yet it deceives those who indulge it, because often uttered seriously, and because fostering the expectation of future amendment. But the worst of all devils is the devil who, to gain his purpose, puts on the garments of an angel of light. He is emphatically the Deceiver. By the hook whose barb is concealed under the gilded bait of future amendment, he draws souls to perdition. Infidelity

and open wickedness have slain their thousands, but "I hope my time will come yet" has slain and is slaying its tens of thousands. Through every day on which the sun shines upon our world, it is making fearful additions to the number of the lost.

2. It teaches us the deceptiveness of this hope. "I hope my time will come yet." No time is fixed. No resolution is made. Every thing is left indefinite. No barriers are thrown up against the encroachments of sin. No position is taken against the wiles of the adversary. And all this time depravity is fortifying itself in the heart, and Satan is multiplying the cords that bind us to sin, and is casting up new difficulties in the way of our return to God. "I hope my time will come yet." And that time, like the hour of death, is a retreating point before us. It seems equally distant at sixty as at twenty. Like that luminous meteor, the ignis fatuus, the offspring of corruption, which retreats before its pursuers, and which allures them to destruction, it retreats as rapidly as we follow it. It is as far before us in old age as in youth. When our feet are upon the crumbling verge of the stream of death, it is flaming brightly on the opposite bank. In our pursuit of it we fall into the stream, and, after a few fruitless struggles to reach the shore, we are carried down into the ocean of eternity.

And this is the deceptive hope which many are indulging. And although it deceives from youth to manhood, and from manhood to old age, how few, oh how few expel the deceiver! How rarely we again trust the man that has deceived us once, and yet we rely upon this hope, which has only deceived us for threescore years and ten, as implicitly as if it had fulfilled to the letter all it ever promised! Indeed, it so bewitches man that he is absolutely pleased with the dexterity with which he cheats himself out of heaven, by putting off repentance to a retreating point which he never reaches. It only asks for the present, it ever points to the future; it asks for to-day, and points to to-morrow; it asks for this year, and points to the next. And thus, by piecemeal, it cheats us out of all time, and finally hurls us, without repentance and unprepared, into eternity. Dear reader, are you one of those who indulge this fallacious hope? Oh, expel it from your bosom, else it will prove the assassin of your soul!

3. It shows us the importance of improving the present time to secure the great end of our existence. That end is the salvation of the soul and the glory of God. If the soul is lost, life is a lost adventure; if the soul is lost, all is lost. Hence the emphatic, the infinite importance of the precept of the Savior, "Seek first the kingdom of God and his righteousness." The due improvement of present advantages is the great lesson which God and the world are teaching their votaries. God says, as to the soul, "Now is the accepted time." "To-day, if you will hear his voice, harden not your hearts."

But, instead of obeying the command of God, will you yield rather to your own sinful inclination, and say, "I hope my time will come yet?" If so, remember the case of my aged friend, which I have here spread before you. This delusive hope may decoy you onward from youth to middle life, thence to old age. And when the curtains of this life are dropping around you, and when your frail tabernacle is just returning to the dust, even then you may be left to the ineffable folly of saying, "I hope my time will come yet." And without seeing the time for which you hoped, and without the needful preparation to meet God in judgment, you may be ushered into a rayless, hopeless eternity, to be a homeless wanderer from the light of the universe forever.

Put not off present duty to an uncertain future. Act in the present and for the future. Fix not even a time in the future for repentance. This is boasting of to-morrow. You may never reach it; or if you do, there may be no desires after God. Or you may have desires—you may lift up your sails to catch the wind of heaven, but there may be no celestial breezes to fill them, and you may have to lie down in everlasting sorrow. As you value, then, the life of your soul, say not, oh say not, "I hope my time will come yet."

THE DYING REGRET OF HARRIET.

Harriet B—— was a teacher in my Sunday-school, and although not a professor of religion, she was far more punctual and faithful to her duties than many that were. She was a member of my Bible-class, and was among its most intelligent and interested members. Soon after I became her pastor, attracted by her serious deportment and intelligence, I sought an interview with her for religious conversation. Although remarkably diffident, she expressed a feeble but intelligent hope in Christ. She thoroughly understood her demerits as a sinner; she had the clearest views of the way of salvation through the atonement and righteousness of Christ; she fully comprehended the great truth, that faith is the saving grace; and she hoped she did believe in Christ.

Having ascertained this to be her state of mind, I placed before her her duty to connect herself with the Church of God. She expressed her great unworthiness of such a privilege, and her great unfitness for communion with the saints. She spoke much of her remaining corruption, of her varying feelings, of her besetting sins; and she expressed it as her conviction that none should attach themselves to the Church until they were assured of their good estate. I strove to instruct her upon the difference between faith and assurance. She soon comprehended me, and feeling that I had gained my point, and that at the next communion, which was then near, she would profess faith in Christ, the interview closed.

The communion season came and passed away, and Harriet, as usual, was only a solemn spectator of the solemn scene. Repeatedly had I interviews with her similar to that now narrated, and at the close of each I indulged the hope that at the next communion season she would connect herself with the Church. But these hopes, often indulged, were as often disappointed. Her fidelity to her Sabbath-school class—her regularity in attendance upon all the means of grace—her readiness to do for the cause of Christ, never intermitted; but communion seasons and years passed away without her confessing Christ before men.

Late on a summer evening, I was called from a social circle of Christian friends to see Harriet before she died. She was seized with a fever, which, before it was feared, had almost extinguished life; and before she passed away from earth she desired one more interview with me. Her dying chamber presented a scene never to be forgotten. The family, save her mother, who had previously passed into the skies, were around her bed, and, with a mind clear and collected, she was rapturously speaking to them about Jesus, and the glory, honor, immortality, and eternal life which he had purchased for all that believe in him; and with a propriety and earnestness that I have never known surpassed, she exhorted them all to believe and to obey Christ. Never did I witness such a change.

The diffident, retiring female was now all confidence; the tongue that was almost dumb now sweetly and delightfully sung; the trembling hope was exchanged for assurance and joy, and the hand which she dared not put forth to partake of the elements of the broken and shed blood of Christ, was now extended to grasp the crown of glory.

When the excitement of addressing her impenitent friends had passed, and she had recovered a little from the exhaustion, I took my seat by her side, and held with her my final interview until we meet in glory. Her confidence in Christ was strong and cheerful. The clouds which, like dark curtains, had so long hung around her mind, had all passed away, and the light of the Savior's countenance shone upon her with the brightness of the sun in its strength; and after requesting me to preach a sermon to the young, after her burial, on the text, "Prepare to meet thy God," she uttered, with the deepest emotion, the following memorable sentiment: "Would, would, oh would that I had taken your advice, and that I had confessed Christ upon earth! I hope to enjoy him forever in glory; but from the joy and from the bliss of having confessed Christ before men, I am now, and shall be forever, excluded. Warn all not to do as I have done." I prayed with her and bade her farewell. Soon afterward the silver cord was loosed, the golden bowl was broken, and her spirit rose up to the God that gave it.

This narrative has deeply impressed upon my mind a few truths, which I desire to place upon record for the prayerful and serious consideration of every reader.

1. Many, very many are prevented from professing Christ before men because they discriminate not between faith and assurance. Here was the practical error of Harriet, and which for years kept her from the communion of the saints. Faith is believing what God has said to be true, and treating it as true; assurance is the persuasion that I do believe—that I am a Christian. These are very distinct. Faith is trusting in Christ for mercy; assurance enables us to say, I know I believe. The great prerequisite for professing Christ before men is a cordial belief in Christ, and not the assurance that we are Christians. Reader, are you in the state of mind of her whose brief narrative I have here placed before you? Do you believe in Christ? Then wait not for assurance to profess Christ before men. With the delightful persuasion that Christ is mighty to save, willing to save, waiting to save, all that believe, go and devote yourself to his service, and follow him in the way, and assurance and all the other graces which grow along the path of obedience will be yours in due time.

2. Many are prevented from professing Christ because of wrong views of the prerequisites to such a profession. It is the superficial and unconverted that usually press their way into the Church; the serious and sober, to whom God has revealed what is in their hearts, usually, like Harriet, are found waiting at the gates, and watching at the posts of the doors, anxious to enter in, but yet afraid, lest all may not be right. She felt her unworthiness of such a privilege; but who are worthy? She felt unfit for the communion of the

saints; but who are fit? And are not the best and holiest members of the Church, like ourselves, imperfect? She spoke of her remaining corruption, but so did Paul; and of her varying feelings, but so did David; and of her besetting sins, but these had all the saints. It is far better to feel unfit than fit—unworthy than worthy. Christ came, not to call the righteous, but sinners to repentance. It is they who are sick that have need of the physician. It is the weary and heavy-laden that Christ invites to himself for rest. Reader, is the question before your mind, Shall I or shall I not profess Christ before men? As you would do duty intelligently, and follow Christ truly, I implore you to permit nothing to enter into its settlement but that which truly belongs to it. Do you feel that you are a sinner? Do you feel that Christ alone can save you? Do you feel that you can rest alone upon him for salvation, as he is offered to you in the Gospel?

"Let not conscience make you linger,
Nor of fitness fondly dream."

Go and join yourself to the people of God, and follow Christ in all the paths of duty, and your light will become brighter and brighter even unto the perfect day. To profess Christ before men, the great prerequisite is a true and lively faith in him. Let all of whom believing and doubting Harriet is the representative, ponder this truth, until they see it in the broad light in which it is written on the pages of the New Testament.

3. Let none think that they can serve Christ as fully, and possess the joys of salvation as abundant-

ly, without professing him before men, as by so doing. This position, though often asserted, is utterly false. It involves a general principle which lays the axe at the root of the Church as a divine institution. If one may serve Christ fully away from the Church, so may all; and if all adopt this principle, what becomes of the Church? It passes away from the earth in two generations.

Besides, obedience is better than sacrifice, and the test of true obedience is to follow the Lord fully. Can we so follow him away from his Church and people, when we have the opportunity to join them? Is there a solitary case to be found among all the records of men in proof of this? Who, on their dying bed, have ever rejoiced that they served Christ disconnected with his Church? I have known many who attempted to do this, and in every case I could trace it to a latent desire to serve God and mammon. And the Savior tells us this is impossible.

The dying Harriet felt, when trembling on the confines of eternity, that her failing to confess Christ before men would subtract from her joy forever. And she felt truly. One of the most precious promises of the Savior is made to those who confess him before men. And I feel that I should be disobedient to her dying injunction, unless I lift my voice, warning all men every where against those errors which, dying, she deplored. There are consolations in Christ which none can truly know, here or hereafter, but those that follow the Lord fully.

4. Harriet died in her youth, and while putting off

a present duty to a future day. That future day she never saw, and the duty was never performed. And before she entered the chariot which conveyed her to glory, she felt, and she said, that her song of praise to the Redeemer must be lower than the song of those who confessed Christ amid many tribulations, who washed their robes and made them white in the blood of the Lamb. Reader, do duty to-day. Your highest duty is to follow Christ — so follow him as you will wish you had done when you come to die. These truths are addressed to you from the death-bed of Harriet.

"BUT I WAS NOT ONE OF THEM."

I am one of those pastors who continue the good old apostolical practice of visiting "from house to house" among my people; and although a most laborious, it is an exceedingly important and efficient way of doing good. It gives access to minds and hearts that can never be reached from the pulpit; it tends to bind pastor and people together, and it is richly suggestive of topics for public instruction.

On a damp and chilly day in the month of November, I went forth on a pastoral visitation among my people. It was my first regular visitation after my settlement among them. As the day was drawing toward its close, I entered a farm-house wearing externally and internally an air of comfort. Every thing was in pleasant preparation for my reception. On either side of a glowing fire sat the father and mother of the household, now well advanced in years; and ranged between them were the other members of the family, the youngest child, then a lad of about fifteen years, holding his catechism in his hand. He could repeat it from beginning to end, showing that, as to the theory of religion, his education was not neglected. I went round the family group conversing with each as to their personal interest in the work of Christ for the salvation of men. Every thing was free, social, and pleasant; but while with an intelligent understanding of the plan of salvation, and while freely admitting that there was no way for them to heaven but through faith in Jesus Christ, I found, to my great grief, that parents and children were aliens from the commonwealth of Israel. After giving to each a word of instruction adapted to their circumstances, and to the views expressed by them in conversation, we bowed together before the high and lofty One; and having implored for them all temporal and spiritual good, I bade them farewell.

The father, whose natural strength many years had not impaired, and whose kind and gentle manners made him a favorite among his neighbors, followed me to the door, and, closing it after him, stopped me on the porch. His countenance gave strong indications that there was something pressing upon his soul which he wished to communicate. Hoping that the Holy Spirit had blessed my visit to his conviction, I waited with anxiety to hear what he had to say. After a considerable pause, taking me by the hand, he thus addressed me:

"I thank you for this visit; although the first you have made us, I hope it will not be the last. I thank you for all the advice you have given us; and as you have but just commenced your labors among us as a minister, I wish to give you a word of advice, based on my own experience. Let us old people alone, for we are hopeless subjects, and devote your labors to the youth of your flock. Forty years ago, when Mr. A—— was our pastor, I was greatly anxious about my soul. Many were then converted, but I was not one of them.

During the ministry of Mr. M—— I was often greatly anxious about my soul—I went to the conference-meeting—many were converted in the successive revivals enjoyed, but I was not one of them. And now, for years that are passed, I have not had a single feeling on the subject. I know that I am a lost sinner—I know that I can be saved only through Jesus Christ—I feel persuaded that when I die I shall go to hell forever—I believe all you preach—I believe all you have said to me and my family, but I feel it no more than if I were a block of marble; and I expect to live and to die just as I am; so that my advice to you is to leave us old people to ourselves and our sins, for you can not do us much good, and devote yourself to the work of seeking the conversion of the young."

And all this, and more, was said with a kind and pleasant bearing, which forbade every thing like suspicion of his motives; and yet with a cool deliberateness which made me feel that the man was a mystery. After placing before him the fullness of the redemption which is in Christ Jesus, we parted.

I remembered the incident, and watched the progress of this man. His seat was rarely vacant in the sanctuary. To hear the word preached, he breasted many a storm which kept the professor of religion at home. I made him other visits; and while he admitted all I said, and freely confessed his lost state, I never witnessed in him the slightest ruffle of religious emotion. He was a true prophet of his own fate. He lived as he predicted, and so he died. And we laid him down in a hopeless grave, after having spent his threescore years and ten without repentance toward God, or faith in our Lord Jesus Christ, in the midst of a congregation over which God has often made windows in heaven.

The lessons taught by this incident are very obvious, highly important, and deeply impressive. To a few of these, the prayerful attention of the reader is earnestly requested.

Are you advanced in life? Are you approaching the verge of old age? Then ponder, unless you are a Christian, the many probabilities that you will never be converted. "Can a man be born again when he is old?" Being long habituated to certain ways of thinking and doing, the aged find it difficult to change. Old ways and things become, to a certain extent, sacred. Hence their attachment to old modes of dress and of living—to old habitations and associations. The old heathen die as they live. The aged papist dies as he lives. The most gross absurdities of his system of worship become interwoven with his feelings on the subject of religion, and form the most sacred part of it; and the aged moralist, infidel, atheist, die as they live. Custom renders every thing easy; and the man who, through a long life, has been accustomed to hear and to assent to the truth of heaven with indifference, will, to a moral certainty, die as he lives. His habits are to him what his skin is to the Ethiopian—what his spots are to the leopard.

And the ground of the moral certainty that you will not be converted lies not in God, but in yourself. God is ever waiting and willing to be gracious; but you have been so long accustomed to neglect every call to work out your salvation, that there is no probability that you will now attend to it. But, although your feet are on the borders of time, you have only to look to Jesus in true faith to be prepared for eternity. At the eleventh hour of your life, the Gospel puts the cup of salvation into your trembling hand. Oh hasten to drink it, remembering that this hour is on the wing, and that, when it ends, you will be in the grave, where there is no work, nor device, nor knowledge, nor repentance.

Are you one of that large number who have been often convicted of sin without being converted? who have been often deeply impressed with divine truth without receiving " with meekness the ingrafted word which is able to save your soul?" If so, then yours is an alarming state. You are passing through that process which has converted many a tender heart into a heart of steel. Of this process there are many illustrations. The young physician is excited, perhaps disgusted, the first time he witnesses a dissection; but he will soon use the knife upon the living or dead subject without the least emotion. The young soldier, when he first treads the battle-field, is filled with fear and trepidation; but in the course of time the clangor of the war-trumpet is to him the sweetest music, and the field of his highest glory is the field of blood and carnage; and in a similar way, the heart that melts under the preaching of the Gospel, and that trembles at the word of the Lord, becomes as hard as the flint, and as unimpressible. This state is gained by slow stages. Satan does not permit the heart to offend the judgment by asking too much at once. He asks but here a little and there a little. And, by degrees, the judgment is perverted, and the conscience is seared, and fear is overcome, and the warnings of God's word and providence lose their point and power, and the most awful truths of heaven, whose reality the mind never questions, fall as lightly upon the soul as does the snow-drop upon the rock. Thus we pass on from youth, when the feelings, like the bosom of the ocean, are ruffled by the slightest zephyr, to old age, when the feelings are like the Dead Sea, whose surface can scarcely be excited by the sweeping whirlwind, and which, if excited, soon relapses into its sullen stillness. And the longer the process is continued, the harder the heart becomes. If religious impressions, often made on your mind, have been as often erased, yours is a fearful state. If the slightest whisper of the Spirit yet calls you to the cross, go at once, lest, when that whisper dies away upon your ear, the Spirit may take its flight, saying, "He is joined to his idols; I will hereafter let him alone." This will be sealing the instrument which consigns you to eternal death.

Are you yet in your youth, with the dew of the morning of your life sparkling on your green leaf? Then has this incident a most important lesson for you. If difficulties, many and great, impede the conversion of the aged, how important to secure your salvation while young! Many promises are now in your favor, but they are daily diminishing. Your heart, now easily impressed, is becoming harder and harder. You are now comparatively but little occupied with the world, but it is throwing daily a new fold around you. You should not be ignorant of the important truth that the probabilities of your salvation are becoming fewer and weaker as your years roll on. It is an easy matter to break up the earth in April and May, and to plant in its bosom the good seed that bears fruit in autumn; but what power can cultivate it when congealed by the cold, and covered by the snows of December? Seize, oh seize, then, the halcyon days of youth to prepare for old age, death, and eternity. Wait not until covered by the rust, and weakened by the infirmities of years. To-day, if you will hear His voice, harden not your heart. Opportunity, grace, mercy, heaven, eternal glory, are all upon the wing of the present hour; condemnation, hell, eternal despair, the worm that never dies, may all be in the train of the next. So improve your youth as not to be left to say in old age, "Many were converted, BUT I WAS NOT ONE OF THEM."

LAURA ANN.

It was the afternoon of the week for my family visits. A cold November storm was brewing, and amid the unpleasant and chilling drizzle by which it is often preceded, myself and elder went forth to our duty. Regarding the church as the centre of the parish, my custom is to commence my visits with the most distant families, and to visit toward the centre. As we passed along, I observed a parishioner cutting wood in his yard, and sought in vain a nod of recognition. Little did I suspect the train of thought which was passing through his mind. We soon reached this family in the regular order of visitation, and found every thing ready for our reception. The parents were not pious; and Laura Ann was about four years old, sitting at her mother's knee. They admitted the importance of religion; they confessed belief in all its doctrines; they had no excuse to offer for remaining in a state of impenitence. The duty of immediate repentance and of faith in Christ was urged, and having obtained a promise of immediate attention to personal and family duty, we prayed with them and retired; and of this interview Laura Ann was a youthful but apparently absorbed witness.

On the next week we met these parents at a prayer-meeting at some distance from their residence. There was an obvious change in their appearance and demeanor. The countenance of the one was cheerful and hopeful—of the other, confiding, but shaded: both were hoping in Christ. On the day of that family visit they had committed themselves to God, and erected the family altar, and had resolved to serve the Lord as long as they lived. When chopping wood, he saw me pass his house: he had arranged in his mind what to say to me when I returned to make my visit—he would give this excuse, and then that; but by the time I reached his house, every excuse was given up one after the other, and when the interview took place, he frankly confessed that he was a sinner, and without any excuse for his impenitence. They found Christ at the same time, connected themselves with the Church at the same time, and they yet live, proving by a simple, humble life of obedience that the Lord created a right spirit within them.

The delicate, sedate, and thoughtful appearance of Laura Ann, as she grew up from childhood to youth, greatly interested me. When examining her in the Catechism, and explaining to her the way of life through Jesus Christ, I have seen her whole mind absorbed, and her eyes often suffused with tears. Before she was twelve years of age, the disease which had marked her for an early grave made its appearance. She was withdrawn from school, and was soon confined to the house and to her room. On my first visit to her bed of sickness, I was greatly interested in her state of mind. She felt that she must die, and her great anxiety was to have a true preparation for her change. I briefly explained to her the plan of salvation through Christ. She felt she was a sinner—she knew and appreciated the great truth that Christ Jesus died for sinners, and would save to the uttermost all that would believe in him; and she felt that she could believe on him to the saving of her soul. And yet she felt that she was not a Christian. But when I simplified the way of life, and placed before her what it was that constituted the Christian, and gave a true ground for hope in Christ, a cloud seemed to pass away from her sky, and she said, "If this is so, I think I can say, 'Lord, I believe, help thou my unbelief.'" I believe she had been previously converted; and before my first visit to her bed of sickness was ended, she had a comforting evidence that she was a child of God.

Her disposition was the most confiding, simple, and child-like. Her disease slowly progressed to its termination, as if for the purpose of permitting her graces to grow and to bear fruit; and from the first hour of her expressing a hope in Christ until the silver cord was loosed and the golden bowl was broken, her confidence was as firm as the truth upon which it was based, and her hopes as bright as the promises which inspired them.

Sitting by her bedside, she said to me, "While I know that there is nothing saving in Church connection, and that I shall never be able to go out from this room to commune with the people of the Lord at the Lord's table, yet I would be greatly gratified to confess Christ before men, and to identify myself with his visible people." I told her that her desires could be gratified in these respects; and a smile of joy immediately lit up her pale countenance. A committee from the Session went to her sick-room, one of whom was an aged and venerated man, deeply read in a Christian experience. They united in stating to their brethren that a more interesting or satisfactory evidence of love to God they had never heard from young or old. And she was received to the communion of the saints, although unable ever to meet with them in the breaking of bread; and the fact of her connection with them was an unfailing source of comfort to her.

Her uncomplaining submission to the will of God was remarkable. Instead of fretting under the hand of the Lord, or complaining that she was sick when others of her companions were well, she was often heard to rejoice that she was so early attacked with consumption. "It is a protracted disease," she would say, "and gives me time for preparation and examination; and it has come early in life, before strong attachments and ties to earth were formed." Often have I heard her say, "I can not be too thankful that I am dying of consumption."

Her solicitude as to her parents was of the most deep and delicate character. Often afflicted with hemorrhage, she concealed the blood in cloths about her bed, and had them removed without their notice. When asked why she did so by her mother, her reply was, "I could not bear to see you suffer the pain which these repeated evidences of my incurable disease gave you." A portrait of her, by an artist in the town, was suggested, to which she readily consented, and solely on the ground that "it may be a comfort to my parents when my body is in the grave—when I will be present no more to comfort them." And when these parents would sit sorrowing by her side, she would enter with them into the most sweet and earnest conversation, to reconcile them to her sickness and early death, and to prove to them that for her "to depart and to be with Christ was far better" than to remain on earth, and to jeopardize her salvation amid its cares and besetting sins. And she succeeded in her efforts; for never did parents more tenderly love a child, or more cheerfully surrender one when God called her away.

Her cheerful piety, scarcely shaded by a single cloud of doubt, rendered her sick-room very attractive. As her pastor I was often there, and never without receiving at least as much instruction as I imparted. "You often feel, I suppose, Laura," said I to her, "a desire to recover, and to serve God by a life of active obedience." She promptly replied, "Upon that subject I have no desire or will. I refer all to God. I am afraid, if I should get well, I might lose my hope and confidence in Christ;" and after a brief pause, caused by weakness, she ended the sentence, saying, with a look and tone never to be forgotten, "I would rather have my hope than my health." Christ and his cross was her ceaseless theme, and that not in a forced way, but in a manner the most easy and free. Her words and feelings were as natural as the waters coming up from a living spring. Shortly after her reception into the Church, she was visited by a pious female, who failed to say any thing to her on religious matters, at which she expressed great surprise. She greatly delighted in the visits of an aged elder, whose life for many years had been hid with Christ in God, and who never retired from her room without feeling that he was the one edified and benefited.

Her meditations often took the direction of recognition in the spiritual state. She sought my opinion upon the subject, which served to confirm her in her own previous conclusions. Thenceforward she was confirmed in the belief of the mutual recognition of the blessed in heaven; and the belief she used as a source of consolation to herself and of comfort to her friends. To an aunt, who, in retiring from her room, asked her what she would say from her to her cousins, she replied, "Tell them that I expect soon to meet Sarah Ann in heaven." Sarah Ann was a cousin who had died but a short time before in the triumphs of faith.

With great intelligence she marked, for months, the progress of her disease. When her feet began to swell, she remarked, "The struggle, thank God, will now soon be over." "My Church, and minister, and the people," she said, "are very dear to me; I wish to be buried in that grave-yard, where my parents can visit my grave, if they wish, when they go to church on the Sabbath." She now made distribution of her little effects to her friends, to be kept as memorials of her when she was gone. To a younger brother, who has since been laid by her side, she gave a Testament, in which she ordered the following lines to be transcribed, written with her own hand:

"MY DEAR BROTHER,—You are young, but you have a soul to save. Pray every day, and read this little book. Pray for a new heart, and that you may be prepared to meet me in heaven. Remember your dying sister, LAURA."

For a young sister she laid aside a Sabbath-school book, and wrote the following lines, to be written in it after her death:

"MY DEAR SISTER,—If it is your wish to meet me in heaven, you must prepare. We soon shall part: shall we ever meet again? Prepare to meet thy God. Remember the dying words of your sister

"LAURA."

To a cousin she wrote,

"I feel that I must soon take my departure. Oh, what a sweet thing to be resigned to die! I feel that I can put my entire trust in Jesus my Redeemer.

"LAURA ANN."

Having made distribution of her articles, she felt she had then nothing to do but to die, and then "to go home to heaven." Looking out from her window, she said, "I know I shall never walk these streets more, but I shall soon walk the streets of the New Jerusalem." On being asked whether she was willing to leave all her friends, she replied, with spirit and energy, "O yes; the enjoyments of this world are nothing in

D 2

comparison with the enjoyments of heaven." Waking from a deep slumber on the last Sabbath morning of her life, she exclaimed, "How lovely every thing seems! It reminds me of a picture I once saw of the bright, bright path that leads to heaven." Remaining for some time in a silent and thoughtful position, she was asked why she said so little to her afflicted friends around her. She replied, "I feel that I have been visited by angels, and I long to be away with them." When the last sands in the glass of life were running, a relative whispered in her ear, "This is death; the struggle will soon be over." She replied, with a smile lighting up all her countenance, "God is good;" and in a few moments afterward her spirit returned unto God who gave it. Her life was a brief one; it had not quite reached fifteen years, but she attained the great object of life, and its end was glorious. No more lovely life or death have I ever witnessed.

How manifold and important the lessons of this narrative!

Does it not illustrate the importance of ministers retaining the good old plan of family visitation in the Churches? In the pamly days of the Church, the pastor, with his elder, regularly visited the families of his charge. He conversed personally with every adult; he catechised the children — he prayed with them. Thus, while not failing in his duties in the pulpit, he carried the Gospel from house to house. Not a family was overlooked—not a person, young or old, was neglected. A personal appeal was made to every individual, and a bond of union, which death only could sever, united pastor and people; and a piety, less showy than in our day, but far more solid and consistent, was the result. To that family visit, under God, we trace the conversion of the parents of Laura Ann, and subsequently her own brief but bright life and happy death. Family visitation is a most laborious, but a most important part of a pastor's duty; in the neglect of it, we know not how any man can feed the flock of God.

Does it not illustrate the importance of the religious instruction of the young? Laura Ann, from childhood, knew the Holy Scriptures, and was instructed in the Shorter Catechism; not in a forced, but entirely simple and natural way, she was accustomed to religious conversation. These things made deep and early impressions, and, through the agency of the Spirit, resulted in her early conversion. Oh, how important the precept, "Train up," or, as it is in the margin, "Catechise a child in the way he should go." The lovely life and happy death of Laura Ann were intimately connected with her domestic religious instruction. When family religion is rightly maintained in every Christian family, it will be scarcely second to the ministry in its influence in extending the dominion of Christ in our world.

To those in youthful years, does it not illustrate the importance of the precept, "Remember now thy Creator in the days of thy youth?" While the dew of her youth was sparkling upon her green leaf, the hand of Death was laid upon Laura Ann. Her sun set before it reached its noon; but it rose in another sphere, never again to set, where it will shine with unsullied brightness forever and ever.

"Grace is a plant, where'er it grows,
Of pure and heavenly root,
But fairest in the youngest shows,
And yields the sweetest fruit."

THE SCENE IN A GRAVE-YARD.

I WAS asked to visit a young man who was very sick. I was soon at his bedside. Although hitherto careless about his salvation, I learned that he was the son of a praying mother, who had passed into the skies, and who had left her impress upon the hearts of her children. This inspired me with hope, as it gave me a strong hold on the sympathies and conscience of the dying youth before me.

His disease was consumption—the most deceptive of diseases—which, while it is undermining the citadel of life, unfurls the flag of hope from its summit. For months he had struggled against its gradual and stealthy advances, but with wasted energies he now lay gasping for breath before me. I spoke to him of death, but he hoped soon to be well again. I told him of the uncertainty of life, even as to those free from disease; he replied that he had been sick before, and that his youth was in his favor. I spoke to him of the need of preparation to meet death at every moment of his being; he said he hoped his time would come yet. And in this way he closed every avenue of access that I sought to open to his heart.

I finally ventured to ask him if he remembered any thing of his sainted mother. His eyes soon filled, and after a protracted pause, he replied, "Oh yes." I asked him if she ever prayed for him. "Often," was his answer, and with deep emotion. I then stated to him the privilege of being the son of a sainted mother, the blessing of having her yet unanswered prayers on record in heaven for him, and the way of salvation through a Savior. His attention was awakened; and after committing him in prayer to the Lord, I withdrew, deeply impressed with the whole scene.

My visits were repeated at brief intervals for some months, with varying hopes in reference to his trusting on Christ for salvation. On my last visit to him, I found him sitting by a fire in early summer, and wet with perspiration through the difficulty of breathing. I plainly saw that his last sands were running in the glass of life. I again placed Christ before him in the freeness and fullness of his salvation; I dwelt on the blessed text, "Whosoever cometh unto me, I will in no wise cast out;" and having fully explained that whenever whatsoever sinner went to Christ, he would find gracious acceptance, I urged him, like the dying malefactor, to go in the very extremity of life, and told him that heaven would be his. Feeling it was my last time, I sought to do all my duty.

There sat in the room during this and previous visits a younger brother, who heard, with attention, all that was said; and, as I had an opportunity, I strove to impress him with the importance of seeking God in the days of health and of youth, without yet feeling that any deep emotion existed, save that of sympathy with his dying brother.

Not long after my visit, as I predicted to his friends,

this young man died. The day of his funeral was one of brilliancy and beauty; the trees were in their full verdure, and nature, animate and inanimate, seemed full of life; and a funeral procession on such a day was in utter and doleful contrast with the appearance of the heavens above and of the earth beneath. I lingered in the grave-yard after the burial, while the mourners went about the streets. Fatigued and oppressed by the heat, and by the scenes through which I had passed, I took my seat on a marble slab which surmounted, in table form, the grave of a once-honored citizen; and there, shielded from the sun by an umbrella, I sat musing on future events. My thoughts ran onward to the judgment, and I imagined myself amid the scenes of that day of wonders. I heard the sound of the trumpet; I saw the graves opening; I saw the many beloved friends that I had committed to the dust all around me, rising—the corruptible putting on incorruption, and the mortal putting on immortality. And while pondering who of these ascending ones would take their places on the right, and who on the left hand of the Judge, I heard a movement behind me. Feeling that I was alone, I was startled with the noise; and on turning to see its cause, the brother of the deceased young man, who had been repeatedly a witness of my solemn interviews with him, stood before me. His whole aspect and demeanor were emphatically solemn; they spoke the feelings that were heaving within him. "Do you," said I, in a tone modulated into sympathy with his appearance, "do you want any thing of me?" He was silent. I waited for an answer, determined that he should break the silence. "I have come," said he, after a long pause, "to ask you, What shall I do to be saved?" Never was that question propounded under circumstances more deeply affecting. There was the fresh clay under which the remains of his brother were just laid, and there by its side was the green grave of his sainted mother, and all around us and beneath us were the graves of departed generations. I gave him a seat by my side; and after explaining to him how Jesus was the resurrection and the life, I set myself deliberately to work to answer his question.

Fearing that his feelings were the result of sorrow and affliction because of the death of his brother, and knowing how little permanence such feelings usually possess, I sought to find the cause of his deep seriousness, when the following conversation ensued:

"You ask what you shall do to be saved. How long have you felt that you are a lost sinner?"

"For several months past."

"Then your serious feelings have not been caused by the death of your brother solely?"

"No; I have felt for months that I am a sinner against God, that I deserve eternal death, and that, were I to die in the place of my brother, where God and Christ is I never could go. I have witnessed some of your visits to my brother, and they have tended much to produce the state of feeling which now oppresses me."

Being satisfied that his feelings had a deeper basis than mere sympathy, I explained to him the nature of sin as committed against God, and how the punishment revealed against sin was its just deserts, to all which he gave an intelligent and direct assent. I thought I saw that his was not the sorrow of the world which worketh death.

Having satisfied myself on this fundamental point, I sought next to explain to him God's great remedy for sin, as embodied in that simple and intelligible text, "He that believeth in the Lord Jesus Christ shall be saved." Placing myself in "Christ's stead," I repeated the words, "Come unto me, all ye that are weary and heavy laden, and I will give you rest."

"But what," said he, "is it to come?"

"To come," said I, "is to believe—to act faith in Christ."

"But what," said he, in an anxious tone, "is faith?"

I replied that "faith is believing what God has said, and doing what God commands." And in various ways, both from Scripture and reason, I sought to explain the matter to him.

We walked out of the grave-yard together, and as we separated at its gate, I entreated him to cherish the strivings of the Spirit, and warned him against the effects of quenching them. But while he promised well, knowing the deceitfulness of the heart, and how like unto the morning cloud and the early dew are the impressions made by afflictive providences, my fears surpassed my hopes. Yet I hoped for the best, and prayed for his conversion.

On the succeeding Sabbath he was an earnest hearer of the Gospel. He took his seat in my weekly conference. Soon he saw that Jesus came to save sinners; that he was a sinner, and that Jesus came to save him. He trusted and rejoiced. Promptly, yet quietly, he took his place among the followers of Christ. Since then, years have passed away, through which he lived unto the Lord. Consumption—the disease which desolated his family—laid its hand upon him; and when the last sands in the glass of his life were running, he spoke of the scene in the grave-yard with intense interest. It was amid the graves of the dead he was led first to indulge the Christian hope of eternal life; and when the darkness of the valley of death was collecting around him, that hope was as bright as the sun at high noon. With faltering accents he could say,

> "Amid the darkness and the deeps,
> Thou art my comfort, thou my stay;
> Thy staff supports my feeble steps,
> Thy rod directs my doubtful way."

The lessons of this narrative are many and important.

1. It teaches us the sad tendency of the unrenewed heart to postpone preparation for death. When confessing that preparation is essential and necessary, the carnal heart will frame any excuse to postpone it, and will resist any argument which urges to the making of it now. We have heard the man of fourscore and ten years saying, with a tremulous and almost inaudible voice, "There is time enough yet." And in the case of this sick young man, when his lungs were so far gone as to render breathing only possible; when the labor of breathing was so great as to convert his

whole body into a fountain of tears; when vitality had commenced its retreat from the extremities, and when the silver cords were loosing in every direction, even then was he weaving the web of hope as to the future! Oh, reader, if there is any evil tendency of your heart which should create more alarm than another, it is the tendency to postpone preparation for death to an uncertain future. You are not so much in danger from infidelity, crimson sins, or open resistance to the authority of God, as you are from procrastination. While other sins have slain their thousands, this has slain its tens of thousands. If the Spirit is now striving, now is your accepted time; and the days of sickness or of old age are no better adapted to secure the great end of life than they are to secure any of its less important ends.

2. It teaches us that although we may fail in doing the direct good which we honestly seek, we may be doing a great good indirectly. I sought with earnestness the salvation of that young man when the vulture Consumption was preying on his vitals. And while we can not look behind the curtain which screens eternal things from our view, or know what God's grace and power may effect in the dying hour, yet, as he passed behind that curtain, he left not the evidences of true faith which we all desired. But what was said to him, perhaps in vain, was not lost upon his younger and listening brother. Although the seed fell by the way-side, the ground was prepared for its reception. If my visits were lost upon the dying, they were blessed to the living; and if the good directly sought

was not obtained, perhaps a greater good was indirectly effected. Our ineffective efforts to save some may be blessed to the salvation of others for whom they were not directly intended. The life-boat may bring back others safely to the shore, although the waves may be made the winding-sheet of the friend for whose rescue it was sent out amid the raging billows.

3. It teaches us to preach the Gospel every where. We must sow our seed beside all waters, not knowing which shall prosper, this or that; nor must we reserve our pungent appeals for the crowded church or for the large assembly. Never are appeals made more successfully than to sinners alone. Years have passed since the occurrence of that scene in the grave-yard, but its memories are yet fresh; nor do I remember ever having preached the Gospel with more unction, spirit, directness, or effect, than when that young man was my only auditor, and the tombstone my pulpit. His life and death gave proof that the seed fell in good ground, and its ripe fruits have been collected into the garner.

HELENA, THE MOTHER OF CONSTANTINE.*

CONSTANTINE, surnamed the Great, holds a conspicuous place among the heroes of history. The son of Constantius Chlorus, he was born, as is supposed, in Nissa, in the year 272. Trained to arms from his youth, he served with high distinction in the Persian war under Galerius. Fearing for his personal safety because of the jealousy of Galerius, he fled to Gaul just in time to join the army of his father in his expedition against the Picts in Britain, when he was about thirty-four years of age. Chlorus died in 306, and his son immediately asserted his claim to a share of the empire. This claim was reluctantly acknowledged by Galerius, and with the title of Cæsar he became master of the country beyond the Alps. He took up his residence in Treves, and governed his people with justice and moderation — loved by his subjects and feared by his enemies. Soon, however, he became involved in wars with rival emperors, in all of which his arms were victorious; and by the decisive victory over Maxentius at Saxa Rubra, near Rome, he became sole master of the West in the year 312.

Soon after this, important events took place in the East. On the death of the tyrant Galerius in 311, Licinius and Maximinus divided his empire between

* Written for Appleton's "Women of Ancient Christianity."

them. Their clashing interests soon led them to war, in which Maximinus was defeated. The number of emperors was thus reduced to two, Licinius in the East, and Constantine in the West. Between these also a war commenced, which ended in the complete defeat of Licinius in the two great battles of Adrianople and Chalcedon, and in his entire surrender on the condition that his life should be spared. Thus Constantine became the sole master of the empire, when he transferred the seat of his government to Byzantium, which he called after his own name, Constantinople, or the city of Constantine. Here he reigned in peace until his death, which took place in 337.

The character of this great man is very variously estimated by historians. If some would make him a great saint, others would make him a great sinner. The miraculous interposition of a cross in the air in his behalf, claimed by some, others would convert into an evidence that he was an impostor. Whether he was a Christian or a heathen, a good man or a bad one—whether his so-called conversion was an injury or a benefit to the Church, are yet open questions, and are now no nearer settlement than they were hundreds of years ago. Yet the chivalry of his youth—his promptness in assuming the purple as soon as it fell from the shoulders of his royal father—his victories over Maxentius—his moderation and justice in the West—his successful wars with Licinius—his going up, amid so many difficulties, to be the sole master of the Roman world—his transference of the seat of empire from the West to the East—his founding of a great city, and locating it with so much sagacity, and, above all, his support of the religion of Christ by converting the state from being its persecutor to its patron, give him a fair title to be called "the Great," a term which all Christian history has cheerfully yielded to him.

The fame of the man has rendered posterity attentive to the most minute circumstances of his life, and especially to those which entered into the formation of his character. And as the conduct of a mother is influential, to a proverb, in the formation of the character of her children, the question arises, Who was the mother of Constantine, and what was her manner of life?

On these questions we also find the testimony of history at variance. It would seem as if she were a Briton by birth; but whether she was the daughter of King Coël, "who first built walls around the city of Colchester," or of an innkeeper, is not determined. Butler asserts her royal, and Gibbon her plebeian descent. She became the wife of Constantius while yet only a private officer in the army, and the mother of Constantine. When her son was about eighteen years of age, his father was promoted to the rank of Cæsar, which fortunate event was attended with her divorce, in order to make way for an imperial alliance with Theodora, the step-child of Maximianus. By this event Helen and her son fell into a state of disgrace and humiliation, from which they subsequently arose by the prudence, the justice, the ambition, and the military prowess of Constantine.

When or by what means she became a convert to the Christian faith is utterly uncertain. If some would represent her, in her state of divorce, as training up her son in the ways of religion with the resignation of a Christian matron, others would represent her as a pagan until after the vision or the dream of seeing a cross in the air, which led to the so-called conversion of Constantine. We believe the truth in the case to be, that while her son played a double part, to conciliate the Christian and pagan parties in the state, favoring less and less the pagan, and more and more the Christian, until just previous to his death he submitted to the rite of baptism, at an advanced period of her life Helen became a devout Christian, and, in the way and manner of her age and country, a devotee to the cause which she espoused.

Hers was an age when the tendency was to the outward in the spirit of religion. The sensuous had already made vast encroachments on the spiritual; and the devotion claimed by God, and which should be given to the subduing of all the powers and affections to the obedience of Christ, was consecrated to pilgrimages to sacred places, to the collection of relics, and to the erection and the adorning of churches. From all portions of the earth, men flocked to the places where Christ was born, suffered, and was buried; princes made pilgrimages to the tombs of apostles and martyrs; pilgrims even penetrated Arabia to see the dung-heap and to kiss the earth on which Job had suffered with so much resignation. Helen fully yielded herself to this spirit of her times, and, by her high example and patronage, greatly promoted it. Honored by her son, and the wealth of the empire placed at her command, she devoted her rank and treasures to religious services. Assuming the plainest dress, she mixed with the people, was punctual in all her duties, distributed to the needy of her abundance, erected churches, and contributed largely to enrich and adorn them. When her son became master of the East, as of the West, by the conquest of Licinius, she repaired to Jerusalem, though then far advanced in life, and, as is said, discovered the true cross on which the Redeemer was crucified, laid the foundations of the Church on the hill of Calvary, and manifested her zeal for religion by the most princely benefactions. While traveling with royal pomp throughout the East, she yet displayed great condescension. She was kind and affable to all. She waited, as a servant, at the tables of the poor. The soldiers, the poor, the condemned, were every where the objects of her regard. She returned to Rome, where she lived in the constant performance of acts of piety and charity until her death, which occurred in August, 328; and her ashes are now said to be kept in a rich shrine of porphyry under the high altar of the Church of Ara Cœli in Rome.

Passing over the monkish legends, mainly the productions of the Dark Ages, which narrate her finding of the true cross, the miracle which proved its truth, the wonders wrought by her intercession, which would seem to render her a fictitious personage, we are forced to the conclusion that Helena was a devoted Christian woman. What seems in her character more sensuous

E

than spiritual was the result of the tendency of her age; and what seems in that character disjointed, and of monstrous proportions, and incredible, we must attribute to the imagination of those writers of legends who sought to impress the living by the most unnatural and incredible narratives of the dead. Having embraced Christianity late in life, she sought to retrieve the many years spent in darkness and sin by a consecration of her time, her station, her wealth to the promotion of religion; and her name is embalmed by the entire Church of God, and is worthy of a place among those who have fought the good fight of faith, and laid hold of eternal life. The mother of Constantine is a bright star in that bright galaxy formed by the illustrious women of early Christianity, and whose characters should be held up to every age for the imitation of their sex.

THE FUNERAL AT SEA.

The noble packet ship in which we were to cross the Atlantic was at anchor in the East River. A strong northeast storm had prevented her from sailing on her appointed day, and there she lay, fully equipped for her voyage, waiting favorable winds. The day opened with a brilliant sky and a fine northwester, and at nine in the morning, the passengers, with their friends, were on the deck, when the anchor was heaved, and we commenced our voyage. As we passed down the magnificent bay of New York, I observed among our company a young man of foreign appearance, with sallow complexion, sunken eye, and interesting mien. There was in company with him a young female, who manifested in him the deepest interest, and who only left his side when all friends were ordered into the steamer which had taken us to the Hook. Their parting was most affecting and tender. The young man was a native of Ireland, and, on the advice of physicians, was returning there, to seek, in his native air, a remedy for a deep-seated consumption. A widowed mother was expecting his return home; and the heart of his female friend, on which his image was impressed, was throbbing with anxiety for his return. Both were to be disappointed.

He had taken his passage in the second cabin, and,

as the winds and waves of the Atlantic soon drove us all to our sick-berths, I had lost sight of him for many days, and even his first appearance on shipboard passed away from my memory. When our voyage was about half made, a female, to whom I was a stranger, informed me that a young man in her cabin was very sick, and greatly needed religious instruction. I sent to ask if a visit from me would be agreeable; and being informed that it would be, I hastened to his berth. His cabin was filthy, and filled with impure air; and having not a relative or acquaintance on board, his person, up to this time, was not sufficiently cared for. My interview with him was deeply affecting. He was a child of Protestant parents. On coming to the United States, he had given up all regard for religious things, and lived only for pleasure and the world. A cold had grown into a consumption, which was now near its closing act; and as tenderly as faithfulness would permit, I suggested that, should our voyage be protracted, as there was danger, he might not live to reach his home. The idea struck him with force, and he turned away and wept. On recovering himself, I asked him as to his preparations for death. The answer was full proof of the darkness of his mind as to spiritual things. "Why," said he, "should I fear to die; as I have never done any thing wrong?" I saw at once the need of a protracted visit, and taking my seat on a greasy trunk by his side, I sought to instruct him into the way of the Lord. I told him of our fall—of our native depravity—of the great truth that we are all sinners, and under the sentence of the law, which is death. I then sought by various simple illustrations to fix on his mind a sense of his own sinfulness. Having obtained a no very hearty assent to my statements, I then sought to place Christ before him as the way of escape for sinners, as the only way to heaven; and having placed the Gospel way of salvation fully before him, surrounded by his fellow-passengers in the same cabin, I committed him to God in prayer, and especially implored that the ocean might not be made his grave. The effect upon him I could not well see, but upon others it was deeply solemn. I promised to visit him again.

This visit was early in the week. On the day following he greatly revived, and played cards. The succeeding Sabbath was to be Easter Sunday, and after the manner of those who observe such times and seasons, he commenced his preparations to keep it. With him and others it was to be a jolly day. I sent kind inquiries from day to day as to his health, and asked for another interview, but it was declined for the present. On Saturday I learned he was quite well, and that he hoped to be on deck on Sunday. There was a change in the weather toward the close of the day; the wind increased, and the atmosphere became quite damp. A little after midnight I was called from my berth to do what I could for the dying man. I crowded my way, half dressed, to his berth, where he lay panting away his life. The glaze of death was already in his eyes—the sweat of death was on all his members, and his every sense was closed. He was beyond all aid from man. The scene was deeply affecting. There, on the bosom of the wide Atlantic, at midnight, the winds high, and the billows raging, lay a man, surrounded only by strangers, in the last moments of his existence! Nor were these strangers neglectful of him. Women were there, who, with maternal and sisterly solicitude, ministered to his wants, and wept over his sufferings; and feeling that I could do the dying man no good, I addressed myself to the living. The profane swearer—the card-player—the papist—the infidel were there. But death has power to silence all objections, and to open all ears to serious instructions. I pointed them to the end of all flesh, and to the importance of preparation for it, and we then went together to the throne of God to ask for grace for the dying and the living; and not knowing the hour at which the struggle would close, I retired to my berth, not to sleep, but to ponder the scene I had just witnessed, one of the most solemn I ever beheld. At the dawn of morning it was announced in my state-room that he was no more.

Knowing something as to the superstition of sailors about the continuance of a dead body on board, I made inquiry as to his burial. It was ordered for an early hour, and before breakfast. I asked the captain to defer it until after breakfast, that we might, with all the passengers and crew, have a religious service. He consented. At the hour appointed, the corpse was brought on deck, sewed up in sail-cloth, with a weight attached to its feet, and laid upon a plank, one end of which extended over the side of the ship, and the other rested on the long-boat near the mainmast, thus forming an inclined plane. The flag, with its stars and stripes, covered the capstan, on which lay a Bible. The passengers and crew were all assembled. There were veteran tars and veteran sinners, but all were affected; there were Protestants and papists, but all heard with equal interest. I preached from the text, "And the sea gave up the dead which were in it;" and as the great truths pertaining to the resurrection were unfolded, and as the picture was drawn of the wide sea by which we were surrounded, and whose waves were singing a death-dirge around us, giving up all its dead, a solemn stillness pervaded the mixed congregation. The order was now given to bury the dead, when two sailors gently raised the end of the plank which rested on the long-boat, and the corpse slid into its ocean grave! One plunge, and all was over! It sank to rise no more until the sea gives up its dead; and while it makes but little difference where the body is laid, if the spirit is prepared for its home in the skies, yet there is something forbidding in a burial at sea, which makes it not to be desired. Death at sea is usually not expected there; friends are generally absent; it is away from the sepulchres of our fathers. No mother's tears can bedew our graves; no stone can tell where our dust reposes; no hand of affection can plant the yew, the cypress, or the weeping-willow at our head; no green grass in the spring, an emblem of the resurrection, will ever cover our narrow house. Our bones may rest as quietly as on land amid the pearls and corals of the ocean, but the wide, wild waste above has no attraction. And as the noise of that one plunge sounded through the ship, no doubt the prayer of my lips was the echo of the sentiment of all hearts, "O Lord, if consistent with thy most holy will, let none of my descendants, to the remotest generation, find their grave in the ocean."

This affecting incident suggested many thoughts which I sought to improve to myself and others during the remainder of our voyage.

How varied the disappointments caused by death! In this case, the expectations of a mother as to the return of her son, and of a female as to the return of a brother or lover, were dashed. The idol of their hearts found an unexpected grave amid the billows of the Atlantic! How many such disappointments is death daily making! How the pillars of our houses are falling when apparently strongest! how the lights of our dwellings are going out when shining brightest! how the icy fingers of Death tear in pieces the web of our hope when almost woven! how often it dashes from our hand the cup of blessing as we are raising it to our lips! and yet how rarely we take these disappointments into our calculations as to the continuance of our earthly comforts!

How tender and sympathizing the heart of woman! This young man was an utter stranger to all on board the ship; his conduct was not such as to win the regards of the females in the cabin with him; and yet, when he became unable to help himself, although often grieved by his profanity, they became to him angels of mercy. With a solicitude which increased with the progress of his disease, they watched over him, moistening his parched lips, wiping his pallid brow, rubbing into warmth his chilled extremities, and dividing with him their own little comforts; and when committed to the waves, there was not a dry eye among them all! How like unto the cup put into the hands of the suffering Savior would be the cup of life, were it not for the sweet ingredients infused into it by the kind hand of virtuous woman!

How intensely interesting will be the scene presented by the sea on the sound of the resurrection trumpet! What multitudes lie beneath its waves! On its bosom battles have been fought, and lost, and won; navies have been wrecked, ships have foundered, and by storm, accident, disease, millions have there found a grave. It may be that the ocean covers the antediluvian world, and that the millions who perished in the Deluge repose beneath its waves; and the dead there, small and great, shall rise on the sound of the trumpet! Not one shall be missing from the vast assembly that will crowd around the great white throne! And what a scene will the sea present when, in answer to the trumpet sounding over it, it shall give up its dead! when it shall lift up its waves on high, that those rising from its fathomless depths may pass from their snowy summit into the presence of the Judge!

How needful a constant preparation for death! God is the God of the sea as of the dry land; they equally lie within the kingdom of his providence, and we are equally exposed to death on the one as on the other. Hence the need of a constant preparation for it. We know not what a day may bring forth. At the very hour when this young man expected to be on deck, keeping Easter with his jolly companions, the waves of the Atlantic were made his winding-sheet!

THE LAST GAME OF CARDS.

On my first appearance among my people as their pastor, my attention was strongly arrested by the appearance of one of my hearers. He was an aged man, and his whole exterior evinced that, although moving in the more humble walks of life, he was a character. Although afflicted with the shaking palsy, his step was firm, and, under the circumstances, quick; his countenance was marked, and, although shaded by a massive pair of spectacles, was full of emotion. With his head slightly inclined, he urged his way through the crowded aisle to a pew in front of the pulpit, where he reverently took his seat, and by silent supplication prepared himself for the worship of God; and whatever might be the state of the weather, there he sat on each returning Sabbath, as long as his health permitted, and with the regularity of the sun; and his whole appearance evinced that he was a deeply interested worshiper. His apparent anxiety to hear was greatly increased by a partial deafness; and when the love of Christ was the theme of discourse, the big spectacles were often removed that he might wipe away the falling tear.

I felt anxious to know something about the history of a man whose appearance thus strongly arrested my attention. As I was a new pastor, he was frank, but somewhat reserved in our first interview; but his confidence increased with our acquaintance, and soon he unbosomed to me his whole heart; and the following is, in brief, his narrative, as more than once detailed to me by himself:

He was a youth at the commencement of the war of the Revolution, and not long after its commencement, enlisted in the regular army. He fought nobly in many of its battles, and at the close of the war returned to private life, a thorough adept in almost all the vices of the camp. He drank, swore, and gambled, until he became a proverb for these vices. Thus, with a family growing up around him, he pursued his mechanical profession in a small way, until old age had commenced its encroachments upon him. Notwithstanding his vices, his frank, manly, and decided character always obtained for him respect. His sons grew up in imitation of the father's example, and in the practice of his vices; and many a night did they spend, corrupting one another at the bottle, and cheating one another at the card-table, amid mutual recriminations when they lost or won.

In the winter of 1807 there occurred a storm, which, commencing early in the afternoon, raged with great violence through the night. As there was no exit from the house, the father invited the son to the card-table. Bets were made; and seeing that the son was gaining the advantage, the father ordered the brandy bottle, hoping that by getting his son drunk he might extinguish his wits, and thus come off the winner. For this purpose, while pouring out for his son, he abstained himself. In the proportion the son drank, he became the loser; and, enraged by brandy and his losses, he charged his father with cheating him. A fight ensued, in which the father was the victor; and after first making him drunk, then winning his money, and then severely beating him, he shut up his son in his bedroom.

From the room where that card-table was spread, a feeble light might be seen through the pelting of the storm, sending out its sickly rays through the whole night upon the darkness of the tempest. Having locked up his drunken and beaten son, the father returned to the fire to prepare for his own retirement to rest. And very soon the tempest without was but a faint emblem of that which raged in his own bosom. The question arose, What have I been doing? That suggested another, and another, and another, until the enormity of his conduct was opened in all its crimson folds before him. He saw his vile conduct as a parent in corrupting his own son—teaching him to swear, to drink, to gamble—and in beating him for conduct induced by the poisoned cup which, with his own hand, he put to his lips. His noble soul awoke as from a dream, and he detested it all. His conduct, in its sinfulness toward God, rose up before him, and he abhorred it. He looked forward to the judgment bar, where a strict account should be rendered for his every act, and the terrors of death got hold of him. When he thought of God, he trembled. His neglected Bible was taken down and read. The storm without seemed to increase that which was raging in his soul, and he read, and wept, and prayed, until the morning light. It was his last night at the card-table.

He was not a man to conceal his true feelings. He had been too often at the cannon's mouth and in the deadly breach to fear any body; and the man who truly fears God fears nothing else. A little refreshing from the Lord was at this time enjoyed; and in the morning, crushed and broken in spirit, he went to the minister to ask what he should do to be saved. He was almost received as was Saul when he went up from Damascus to Jerusalem, and "essayed to join himself to the disciples." But, after telling his story, it was seen that the direct hand of God was in the matter, and that he was a subject of the convictions of the Holy Ghost. He was directed into the way of salvation. He was taught, in its true and full sense, that "whosoever believeth in the Lord Jesus Christ shall be saved," and that his sins of crimson dye, of themselves, were no obstruction to his salvation. And after a few days spent as if in the very belly of hell, he found joy in believing. He soon professed his faith in Christ, and for thirty years, without turning to the right hand or to the left, he followed Christ in his ordinances and commandments, and went down to the grave without a spot or blemish on his Christian character. Never did I find him in any other frame than rejoicing in love of Christ—than resting only on his righteousness for everlasting life. And as he had often met the enemies of his country, so he met the last enemy, Death, without a fear, longing to depart, and to be with Christ, which is far better.

But the question will arise, What became of that son, with whom, on that stormy night, he played cards, and had such a disgraceful fight? He was the bane and the sorrow of his father's life. He awoke in the morning to curse his father, and to pursue the evil of his ways. The tears, the confessions, the entreaties of a penitent parent made on him no impression. He lived forgetful of God, an inveterate drunkard, a burden to the community, and died unwept and unregarded; and often have we seen the father's soul wrung with anguish under the bitter reflection that the seeds which were bearing fruit unto death in the heart of that son might have been sown there by his own hand.

How plainly this narrative teaches the following most important lessons:

1. That the means of God for the reclamation of men are exhaustless. One is convicted by a sermon, another by a tract, another by reading the Bible, another by the faithful admonition of a pious parent or friend, another by the examples of the good; but here is a man who is convicted by the very enormity of his sins. God permitted him to follow out the promptings of his depraved heart until he became the corrupter of his own children, a depth of wickedness to which but few descend, and then, by his Spirit, held up that sin before him as an overwhelming proof of his awful depravity, and of his aggravated guilt in the sight of God! We see the hand of God as distinctly revealed on that stormy night in that gambling-room for the conviction of that wicked father, as on the plains of

Damascus in the conviction of Saul of Tarsus. And in view of the infinite variety of instrumentality used by God for the conversion of men, may we not well exclaim, in the language of Paul, "Oh the depth of the riches both of the wisdom and knowledge of God! How unsearchable are his judgments, and his ways past finding out."

2. It teaches us that the sins of men form no barrier to their salvation. This was a sinner of no medium character. Such a character he could not act; the strong elements of which he was formed forbade it. Hence he sinned with a high hand, and without any effort to cloak his sin. He went on until he could corrupt his own children, and make his son drunk, so that he might win his money at the card-table. And yet he found mercy as readily as if he had yielded an external obedience to the moral law from his youth up! God, in his word, seems anxious to illustrate and to reiterate the truth, that though our sins be as scarlet, they shall be white as snow; though they be red like crimson, they shall be made even as wool. Let the wicked, however wicked, forsake their way, and the unrighteous, however unrighteous, their thoughts, and let them return unto the Lord, and he will have mercy on them, and to our God, and he will abundantly pardon. And because it is the nature of sin to beget forgetfulness of the great truth, that "whosoever believeth in the Lord Jesus Christ shall be saved," it can not be too frequently or emphatically repeated in the hearing of all men. If Manasseh, Saul of Tarsus, John Bunyan, and my aged friend, whose history

I have here briefly drawn, found mercy, who need despair?

3. It teaches us to beware of influencing men to evil courses. This father was saved, by the grace of God, from his evil ways; the dominion of sin over him was broken by an almighty hand, but the son that he enticed away from virtuous courses never returned! The cups from which he taught him to drink were never abandoned; the profanity which he learned in his childhood from his father's lips knew no intermission; the father who taught the son to despise religion was, in turn, despised by that son when he became an humble follower of Jesus Christ! An evil course is like an inclined plane, one end of which is on earth, and the other in hell — when men enter on it, they usually slide down to the bottom. As he that turns a sinner from the error of his ways saves a soul from death and hides a multitude of sins, so he that influences a fellow-man to enter an evil course, where acts of sin grow into habits of sin, and where habits of sin give laws to his being, destroys a soul, and becomes a guilty cause of its eternal sinning and eternal suffering! This father and son have gone to the grave, and have gone each to his own place; and if the spirits of the just made perfect in glory do know the fruit which the seeds sown by them on earth have borne unto death, and do mourn over them, how will that father weep amid the bowers of bliss as he contemplates the fate of his son, an eternal outcast from the light of the universe forever, and mainly through his instrumentality! And many parents are leading their children

into vicious courses, whose ends they themselves may escape, but their children never, who have never put the poisoned cup to their lips, and who could never spend an evening with them at a card-table!

THE MORMON PREACHER.

SOUTH of our church, and within less than one hundred feet of it, stands our court-house, surmounted by Justice balancing her scales in the air, and with a flight of steps ascending to its front door. As I was retiring from the church after the close of the service on a Sabbath afternoon, I heard a voice shouting from the court-house steps, which were surrounded by quite a crowd of people. On inquiry, I learned that the shouter was a Mormon preacher, who, in order to secure hearers, took that central stand, and at the hour when my people were dismissed. Of course he had quite an audience, and of just the sort of people which such a creature would attract. I heard not a word of him through the week, but on the following Sabbath, and at the same hour, the scene at the court-house was repeated.

Early in the week after the second Sabbath, I received a letter giving me the information that a Mormon missionary was in our town, and that if I were willing to open our "great temple" for the purpose, he was ready and anxious to debate with me as to the superior claims of the "Latter-day Saints" above those of any other people claiming to be followers of Jesus Christ. It was just such a letter as might be expected from such a learned pundit, and was often made the subject of amusement to my friends and visitors. Of course, it was treated with the silence which it merited.

I supposed that such a man could not find a solitary follower in such a community as ours, but I have since learned not to over-estimate the general sense of any community; and, to my amazement, I soon heard that he had immersed a few persons, members of churches, into the faith of Joe Smith, and that he had taken lodgings in our town. The whole thing was far more amusing than alarming, as it afforded an opportunity, on a very reduced scale, to see who were the stable, rooted and grounded in the truth, and who were the unstable, blown about by every wind of doctrine. There is no absurdity so absurd as to repel all minds, and this ignorant fanatic had his followers.

Meeting two young ladies in the street, they thus addressed me, with considerable emotion: "The Mormon preacher is in this house; he has led after him some of our people: will you not go in with us and talk with him?" I readily accepted their invitation, and the more readily as they were not of my people. The family whose house we entered was a very plain and simple one, poor but honest and industrious, and earning their bread by their daily toil. The man was a cripple, and some sick persons of the family were turned out of the only comfortable room in the house to make way for the Mormon and his wife. I was introduced to him, and while he kept his seat in the corner, I made a polite but cold recognition of the honor. I introduced ordinary topics to try the strength of my new acquaintance. When I got him warmed into a brisk conversational heat, and had taken his altitude, I made nearer approaches to my object by the line of biography, when the following conversation took place:

"Where, sir, are you originally from?"

"I was born and grew up in Canada."

"Were your parents members of any church?"

"Yes; they were Methodists."

"Were you a member of any church before you became a Mormon preacher?"

"Oh yes; I was for several years a member of the Methodist Church, and was a licensed exhorter among them."

"Were you brought up to any trade or profession?"

"Yes; I am by trade a shoemaker, and have worked at it many years for a living, but I had no great love for the business."

"How did you ever become a Mormon from being a Methodist exhorter? The change is a very great one, and should not be made save with deliberation and for good reasons."

"Well, I fell in with a Mormon preacher, and he gave me the Mormon Bible, and I studied it and studied it, until I was convinced that Joseph Smith was a true prophet, and that the Mormon Bible was a true book; and of course I must follow my conscience and judgment. This is the way I became a preacher, and I think, if every body would study the matter as I did, they would believe as I do."

"But Mormonism is not merely a new sect; it is really a new dispensation, is it not?"

"Oh yes, I think it is."

"Think it is! but before you should go round the country to preach its doctrines, and to invite people to believe them, you should be sure; your faith should be without wavering. Do you believe yours to be a new dispensation or not?"

"Oh yes, yes; I believe it is."

"Well, then, the dispensation of the Law, as given by Moses, was introduced by miracles, and so was the dispensation of the Gospel by Jesus Christ. These miracles were the divine testimony to the truth of the dispensations introduced; for that purpose they were wrought and appealed to. Now, if Mormonism is a new dispensation, designed to supplant that of Jesus Christ, it must be established by miracles. We can receive it on no less testimony than that of God, and God gives his testimony by miracles. Do your prophets or ministers work any?"

"Oh yes, constantly; and some of our brethren are great at them," he replied, without faltering or a blush.

"Well, have you ever worked any, and of what kind?"

"Oh yes, several; I have healed the sick, and cured the infirm."

"Very well, you are just the man we want here, as we have a good many of both classes; and here is poor Mr. ———, who has been without the use of his limbs for many years; you can try your hand on him. If you can cure him now, so that he can run without his sticks, we will all believe in you."

He was silent for a moment. He looked at the cripple before him, and feeling that he was rather in a tight place, he replied,

"But he is not a believer."

"Well, but the subjects of miraculous power are not confined to believers, for Christ and his apostles wrought miraculous cures on many that never believed; otherwise we must believe first, and have the testimony afterward."

He looked again upon the infirm man, and thinking that he was a hard case, and feeling that he himself was in a very tight place, he replied,

"We can work cures only on believers."

This he uttered with rather a feeble and crestfallen tone, and obviously feeling that it was nearly all over with him. As if to relieve him a little from his dilemma, but for the purpose of extending my basis for future action, I said,

"But there may be other miracles at which you are more expert than those of curing cripples. Are there any others you can work?"

After pausing for some moments, he replied,

"I only cures the sick when they believe; but my wife, she has the gift of tongues; I have heard her many a time."

This was a little too much, to shift the burden of proof upon the weaker vessel, who was not present, and which I resolved not to permit.

"It is no new thing for ladies to talk with tongues, as the world knows; but with what other than her own tongue does your wife talk?"

"Surely I don't know; I can't interpret, as I am not a learned man; but I have heard her a great many times."

"Did she ever speak in an unknown tongue that any body else could interpret? Can she speak French to the French, German to the German, Irish to the Irish?"

"Not as I know on."

"If, then, you can not understand her, and if nobody else can understand her, and if she can not talk so that any body can understand her, save in her own native English, how do you know—how can any body know that she has the miraculous gift of tongues?"

He was brought again to a dead pause; but, summoning his impudence to his assistance, he said,

"But I know she can speak with miraculous tongues, for I have very often heard her, and so have others."

Having thus driven him to the point of exhaustion, I again turned the subject, and asked him,

"How do you make a living?"

"I depend upon the Lord for my daily bread. He takes care of me; and when I have no money to pay my way, kind friends like these supply my wants."

Forbearance was no longer a virtue. He was obviously a lazy man that hated work, and a low, vulgar impostor, that took up with Mormonism to make a living, after, probably, he had been cast out of the Methodist Church for his sins. And there he had been for some weeks living upon this poor family, because one of its female members had become his follower, and occupying a room from which the sick were excluded to make room for him and his wife of many tongues. Fully believing all this, I thus addressed him:

"My friend, I have no more to say to you. You are a lazy, indolent man—too lazy to make a lawful living for yourself and wife. I advise you to return to the bench and to the last. You are a wicked man; you have laid aside the religion of God, and turned fanatic. You are pretending to powers which you can not exercise, and are thus daily guilty of the sin of blasphemy. You are deceiving people under a Mormon garb, which you simply put on as a cloak for your hypocrisy; and in this way you are living upon poor people who have enough to do to support themselves. My advice to you is to leave the town immediately, or I will send the constable after you as an impostor, living upon these poor people under false pretenses. You are a wicked man, for whom there is no hope, save in repentance for your sins and faith in the Lord Jesus Christ."

He hugged the corner while, with earnestness mixed with concealed mirth, I thus denounced him. He was overwhelmed; he made no attempt to reply. I left the house. He was soon away, with the fear of the constable behind him. I have never heard of him since. For aught I know, he may be one of the pillars of the infernal system of which Joe Smith was the head, and Brigham Young is the tail.

CHRIST NEVER FORGOTTEN.

The theories of philosophers as to memory are various, and often in conflict. While, like hearing or seeing, it is an original power bestowed by God, there are many things in reference to it very mysterious to us. It may be increased to almost any extent. There is on record an account of a man who, after reading a newspaper, could repeat all its contents; and it is said that Cyrus could call all the soldiers of his immense army by name. And it may be impaired to almost any extent, and in a great variety of ways—by diseases, injuries, fright, and old age. William Tennant forgot every thing he had learned, even to the letters of the alphabet, by an attack of fever; and Artemidorus was so terrified by a crocodile as to forget all he ever knew. Nor is there any thing more common in old people than a forgetfulness of passing events, and a vivid memory of the events and occurrences of their youth. Aristotle imputes the shortness of the memory of children to the softness of the brain, which will not hold impressions; and that of the aged to the hardness of the brain, which refuses to receive deep impressions. The old philosophers talked of pictures being made upon the brain, and of the retention of these pictures constituting memory, so that the memory was a great picture-gallery; and as the brain possessed the power of retaining those pictures, persons had a good or bad memory.

I have often felt curious to know, in the case of a failing memory by reason of age, what were the last impressions retained. Dr. Rush tells of a woman who forgot her own name, by reason of the grief induced by the loss of her husband and several children. I have been told of a merchant in New York who had to inquire of those around him, at the window of the post-office, what his name was, before he could ask for his letters; and native-born Germans, who seemed to have lost the use of their own language by a residence of sixty years in America, have been known, in old age, to forget all their English, and to talk and pray only in their native tongue. Facts like these, to any amount, might be stated. I was once collecting from the oldest people facts and incidents for some notes as to the history of the town of my residence, and I was amazed to find with what distinctness and accuracy they could give narrations as to occurrences during the war of the Revolution, when stirring incidents of a few years previous were entirely forgotten; and all this suggested the inquiry as to the impressions longest retained by the mind whose memory is weakened simply by the enfeebling process of increasing years.

On my removal to my present charge, I found among my people an aged woman of peculiar aspect: aged, tall, straight as an arrow, peculiar in her dress, of firm step, with a strongly-marked countenance, she impressed every body at first sight. She walked with a cane, and so straightforward that every body conceded to her the right of way. She went to the end of her seat in the church, whoever occupied its front, and she sat upright through the longest service, hearing and praying over all that was said. Her mental character was like her external appearance, peculiar. Her opinions were defined and firm, and were given without faltering; her likes and dislikes she never concealed. Although possessing considerable property, she lived alone until infirmity rendered a nurse necessary. She survived two husbands, all her children, all her immediate relations, and was like an old tree standing alone in the field while all its former associates had fallen before the axe of the woodman.

She was the daughter of a minister who figured somewhat as a patriot in the war of the Revolution, and was rooted and grounded in the truth. Her education was above the ordinary standard for her time, and served to give emphasis to her character. She was born again during the war of the Revolution, and professed her faith in Christ when the smoke of our battle-fields was passing away before the genius of Peace; and beyond any aged person I ever knew, her memory was retentive and exact as to the men, and scenes, and events of those stormy times. She could describe the features and persons of men, their dress, the very color of their hair; she could give the texts of sermons she had heard seventy years before, and quote sentences from them; and as her social position was such as to bring her into the society of the important men of her youth, she was full of anecdote as to nearly all the men that then guided the destinies of her native state.

But under the pressure of increasing years, her memory began rapidly to fail. In wandering over her rooms at midnight, with a candle, she set fire to her house, and was but just rescued from the flames. She was compelled to remove to another house, and to another part of the town, and thenceforward there seemed to be an almost entire failure of memory. Often I would sit by her side, and naming her first and second husband, I would ask her if she remembered any thing in reference to them. The reply was, No. She had one son, on whose memory and picture she doted, and whose grave she was in the habit of visiting, and who was often the subject of most exciting conversation; but she had no recollection of him. Her former pastor she most tenderly loved, but he was forgotten. She would look into my face, and ask, "Who are you, my child?" I spoke of her father and mother, of her brothers and sisters, but not a trace of them remained. After trying her in these ways until satisfied that on all such subjects her mind was an entire blank, I would ask her, "Do you remember any thing about Jesus Christ?" and she would at once assume an erect position, and her eye would kindle with its accustomed fire, and, seizing my hand, she would say, with her wonted energy, "Can I, a poor sinner, ever forget the dear Savior that has died for me?" And then she would talk with interest for minutes together, and in a most pious and earnest strain, about her dear Savior. When thus excited, I would commence a text of

Scripture, and she would conclude it with perfect accuracy, commencing where I ceased. I would say, "For we know that if our earthly house of this tabernacle were dissolved—" there I would stop, and she would add, "We have a building of God, a house not made with hands, eternal in the heavens." I would say, "There is therefore now no condemnation—" she would add, "To them who are in Christ Jesus, who walk not after the flesh, but after the Spirit." Often did I try her in this way, and never did I find her memory in such a state of torpor as to forget Christ. But as soon as the excitement caused by the name of Christ passed away, she would relapse into her accustomed state of forgetfulness, in which she usually occupied herself in picking out the threads, one after the other, from an old piece of cloth. Thus this once heroic woman would occupy herself for hours together. As it was the first example of the kind I had ever witnessed, it greatly interested me; and as she lived in this state for three or four years, the experiment was very often repeated, and with precisely the same results.

Subsequent to the death of this excellent woman, a similar case came under my notice, and to which I have already referred in these Pencilings. Family afflictions, repeated bereavements, and severe and oft-repeated attacks of sickness, weakened her memory, until her husband, her living and deceased children, were all forgotten—until all traces of the past seemed erased from her mind. Yet the moment the name of Jesus was mentioned, she woke up as from a dream, and after giving utterance to the feelings of her pious soul, she would relapse again into her state of forgetfulness, from which nothing could again rouse her but the name of Jesus.

I met with an aged man during one of my family visitations whose case was one of deep interest. He had passed his ninetieth year, was exceedingly frail, and his memory greatly impaired. He was taught the Shorter Catechism in his youth by a pious mother, and although he had left the Church of his fathers for another branch of the Church of Christ, he instructed his own family in that excellent form of sound words. His children had all passed away, as did nearly all recollection of them. The time was upon him when the grasshopper was a burden, and when he would wake up at the sound of the bird; and his sleepless nights he nearly always spent in asking and answering, in an audible voice, the questions of the Shorter Catechism; and he would go over and over it, from the beginning to the end, without missing a question, and with a perfect verbal accuracy. And yet he could not answer any one question of it if the thread was broken, or if it were asked by another.

These instances, and many like them of which I have heard, have induced me to conclude that the impressions longest retained by a memory failing under the pressure of old age are those of a religious character. In the instances narrated, when parents, husbands, wives, children, friends, were all forgotten, the name of Christ, in all his preciousness as a Savior, was remembered, and texts of Scripture fragrant with his name, and formal statements of Christian doctrine, were repeated as if with unimpaired recollection.

May we account for these statements on the ground that religious truths are those which most engage the powers of the mind and the affections of the heart, and thus most deeply impress both? Or may we account for them on the ground that they absorb more attention, and for a longer time, than any other truths or things with which we have to do? Or is it so that the affections of the renewed heart cling so to Christ, that when these affections are excited, they wake all the memories of his person, work, and love? Or is it so that, amid the sorrowful decays of the powers of the mind, the Holy Ghost is carrying on the great work of sanctifying the soul through the influence of the truth? But, whatever may be the true solution of the above statements, one thing is obvious, that when the minds of the truly pious give out all impressions and recollections of past scenes and events, and of the dearest and nearest friends, even then Christ is in the heart the hope of glory.

Oh, when flesh, and strength, and mind, and memory all fail us, may Christ be the strength of our heart and our portion forever!

THANKFULNESS.

THANKFULNESS is a Christian virtue often commended, and yet but too little cultivated; and how frequently, when thanksgiving is on our lips, is corroding dissatisfaction at the heart! And the fact that God so frequently enjoins a spirit of thankfulness, and the duty of thanksgiving, is a proof of his good-will toward us, and of his desire for our happiness; for while prayer reminds us of our wants and imperfections, and while confession reminds us of our sins and ill deserts, and while repentance brings up in review our violations of the divine law in all their criminality, thanksgiving only exercises the memory on blessings received, and gives a delightful exercise to the affections in view of them. The truly thankful man is the only truly happy man; and while it is difficult to eradicate from human nature a sense of gratitude for benefits received, while even the brute creation, the ass, the ox, the dog, can manifest gratitude, yet none but they who have tasted that the Lord is good can truly thank the Lord for his goodness, or can learn in whatsoever state they are therewith to be content. In the course of a ministry now somewhat protracted, I have met with many, very many fretful disciples, who were evermore complaining that all things were against them, and with but comparatively few who could rejoice in the cloudy and dark day equally as in the day of prosperous sunshine. It is a high Christian attainment, indeed, to feel that all things are working together for our good, when to the eye of sense the very stars in their courses seem to fight against us. Yet one such instance I did find, to the praise of the grace of God.

I called on a family during a spiritual refreshing with which I had but little previous acquaintance. The father was intemperate, and a rampant Universalist, and was far more confident of preparation for heaven than ever was Paul. He was, on the whole, the most full-blown specimen of that enormous error that I had met. He was profane, sharp in intellect, and confident of heaven. The mother was subdued, gentle in her tones, alive to divine truth, and deeply serious, but yet reluctant to give full expression to her feelings in the presence of her husband. Some of the children were deeply-convicted inquirers as to the way to be saved. I soon repeated my visit; and the result was, that that mother, with several members of the family, professed Christ on the same day, and took their seats together at the table of the Lord.

I have met with but few more deeply afflicted than was that excellent woman. Weekly, often daily, had she to bear the presence of a drunken Universalist husband. She was afflicted with the rheumatism to a degree which distorted her joints, and sent excruciating pain through her system, and rendered her often unable to move. Her husband died of a protracted sickness, which rendered necessary all the attention she could render; and it was rendered, amid pain, without a murmur. Two children died, one after the other, with consumption, and in the full maturity of their years; she attended them, as she could, cheerfully and constantly; and, as they died in hope, she committed them to the grave without a murmur. A son, one of the props of her declining years, died in the same way. After covering his remains under the clods of the valley, I called to comfort her as her pastor. But the Comforter abode with her continually; and while she received me with cheerful though sorrowful greetings, she needed none of my aid to lead her to the source of all comfort. Sitting down by her side, we held in substance the following conversation:

"Well, my friend, the Master seems to be wringing out to you a full cup of affliction."

"He is only fulfilling his promises to me," was the reply.

"What promises?" I asked.

"Whom the Lord loveth he chasteneth," was the answer; and she repeated the entire passage with an emphasis and earnestness which showed that she fully understood and applied it.

"But does it not sometimes seem as if you were receiving more than your share of affliction in this life?" I asked. The reply made on me a lasting impression.

"God knows me," she said. "He knows all I need to make me a partaker of his holiness. He will not cause me to suffer a pang beyond what is needful. You speak of my afflictions; why, they are very few; when I commence counting them, I get through in a few minutes; but when I strive to reckon up my mercies, I know not where to begin or end; I can never get through. Many spend their time in going over and over their few afflictions; that does me no good; I strive to count up my mercies, and they make me feel so thankful!" And as she uttered this last sentence, her bent form assumed an almost erect position, and her whole countenance, withered and sunken as it was, and furrowed by many a sorrow, was illumined; it shone as if a flood of heavenly light had suddenly fallen upon it. I was rebuked and instructed.

As she lingered to nearly her fourscore years, amid manifold infirmities, I was her frequent visitor; for months together, a weekly one. Never did I find her complaining—never in any other than a thankful frame. If by any allusion I called her attention to her afflictions, she said just enough to show that she felt them all keenly and deeply, and then turned to her manifold and undeserved mercies, upon which she dwelt with a feeling, at times, approaching almost to rapture. Often would she adopt the language of the 103d Psalm as her own, and exclaim, "Bless the Lord, O my soul, and forget not all his benefits." Although afflicted far beyond the ordinary lot of men, and poor as to this world, she was rich in faith, and was the most thankful Christian I have ever known.

Toward the close of her life, her mind gave way and her memory greatly failed. It was difficult, at times, to rouse her to the point of an interesting conversation. For the purpose of trying her temper and spirit of soul, I would ask her about some of her dear friends; but they had fallen from her memory. I would ask her as to some of the scenes of trial through which she had passed, and under my own eye, but they left no trace behind. I once asked her in reference to her husband and children, but there was no remembrance of them. I then asked her if she knew who was the Lord Jesus Christ, and she started as one awaking from a dream, and went off in a eulogy upon him as her Savior, her Redeemer, who had died upon the cross for her; and after giving utterance to her thankfulness for all his mercies, she relapsed again into a state of forgetfulness; and from the state of mental torpor into which she had fallen, nothing could so arouse her as the name of Jesus. Her entire religious life was one of endurance, strong confidence, and unceasing thankfulness. Although in humble life, she was one of the most instructive Christians I have ever known. Her intellect was bright, but not enlarged by education; her circle was narrow, and with but little in it to excite to high spiritual aspirations; she came into the Church late in life, when the seeds of grace should have been ripening instead of being in the blade; and yet she had, to a remarkable degree, the secret of the Lord—her life was hid with Christ in God. Praise and thankfulness were ever on her lips.

How varied the lessons of instruction contained in this narrative!

How much more disposed we are to complain under the discipline of our heavenly Father than to rejoice in the far more exceeding and eternal weight of glory for which it is all designed to prepare us! And we fret and complain more over the withdrawal of one comfort, than we rejoice over the continuance of a thousand mercies. How this child of God, rejoicing amid privations, should rebuke those who are evermore complaining amid abounding comforts! Alas! how many there are who give convincing evidence that they do love God, and yet who seem ever to say by their conduct that he is a hard master! The precious ointment of grace is in the soul, but it is spoiled by the dead fly of a fretful temper; the true light is in the mind, but it is veiled by a complaining spirit; and when the Lord is leading them to higher degrees of sanctification by ways that they know not, they are evermore saying, "All these things are against me." This can not be otherwise regarded than as a great blemish upon Christian character, and is emphatically reproved by the foregoing portraiture of a dear child of God, whose Christian life was one of deep personal and relative afflictions. Blessed are they who have learned in whatsoever state they are therewith to be content.

It teaches all to cultivate a thankful spirit. Why should a living man complain? And where life is continued, it is usually amid mercies far surpassing all earthly afflictions. The whole Christian economy is designed to call forth abounding thanksgiving; and a Christian is never so truly what his Master would have him to be, nor so like what he will be hereafter, as when, by daily thanksgiving, he is rendering to the Lord according to the mercies he is daily receiving.

There is, perhaps, no better way of cultivating a thankful spirit than by selecting some one eminent for its manifestation, and then seeking to know the mercies which caused his thanksgivings to abound. Such a one was David: so full was his heart, that the least mercy caused it to overflow; so ingenious was he, that he drew a cause of thanksgiving from the most adverse providences of his life. Nothing came amiss to him. "Like the fire which transmutes rotten wood and dingy coal to light and flame," the fire of David's devotion turned his hardships into blessings, and his sorrows into songs of thanksgiving. Such a one was Paul. Feeling that he had all things in Christ, he suffered all things cheerfully, joyfully for his sake, looking forward to the recompense of reward. His life was a continued thank-offering to God for his abounding mercies. No sufferings, persecutions, afflictions, ever drew a complaint from his lips.

And like unto these in kind, if not in degree, was the life of the child of God here narrated. Christ was hers, and she clung to him by a faith which rarely wavered; and, like Paul, she knew that all things were hers; and, with the ingenuity of David, she drew a cause of thanksgiving from her deepest afflictions. And why should not all the children of God be like her? Why should not every believer be in a constant frame of mind and heart which will induce them daily to say,

> "When all thy mercies, O my God,
> My rising soul surveys,
> Transported with the view, I'm lost
> In wonder, love, and praise?"

THE REV. ASHBEL GREEN, D.D.*

Reverend and Dear Sir,—You ask from me my reminiscences of the Rev. Dr. Green, and my views as to his general character as a minister and as a literary man; and while feeling that there are many more competent for the task, because of their long and familiar acquaintance with this great and good man, I hesitate not to comply with your request. I shall arrange my views of his character under a few heads, and bring in my recollections of him by way of illustrating them.

1. He was a man pre-eminently of two characters, public and private; and to form a right estimate of him, he must be known in both. To those who only knew him as a public man, he was stern, unyielding, dictatorial, and repulsive; to those who knew him both in public and in private, he was mild, pliable, and peculiarly attractive. Hence, by one class he was respected, but disliked; while by another he was uncommonly beloved, and regarded as an oracle.

Although I had heard much of him from my boyhood, and had read some of his writings, I never saw him until 1826; and the sight of him, at that time, would induce any young man to resolve to keep at a respectful distance. His form was full and commanding; his appearance was stern; his eye, gleaming

* Written for a forthcoming work of the Rev. Dr. Sprague.

through shaggy eyebrows, was penetrating; his step was firm, and from his cane to his wig there was something, which, to say the least, was more repulsive than attractive to a youth; and with this conclusion agreed many of the anecdotes which I had heard of him while President of Nassau Hall. My acquaintance with him commenced in 1827, and in this wise: Visiting Philadelphia as the agent of one of our national societies, I felt his approbation of my plans necessary to my success. I called to see him, and was introduced into his study. I soon found myself in converse with a courteous, kind, but dignified Christian minister. He not only approved my plans, but tendered his own subscription to the object. Finding, on inquiry, as I was about to retire, that I was a candidate for the ministry, he invited me to a seat by his side; and the impressions made upon my mind and heart by his kind inquiries, by his paternal advice, are vivid to this hour. He dismissed me with his blessings upon myself and my object. Never was a revolution more entire wrought in the feelings of a man, and from that day forward he was my counselor in cases of difficulty; and so pleasant and simple was he in private, that, on leaving my family after an occasional visit of a few days, my little children would cling to his feet and his garments, crying out, "You must not go, Dr. Green." I feel quite sure that those who only knew him in Presbyteries and Synods, and especially in the ardent conflicts of the General Assembly, of which he was almost a standing member, have the most erroneous views of his true character.

2. His was a truthful character. Truth was to him truth; and what he believed he felt and acted out. His was not the policy to believe one way and act another. Such policy he scorned, and withheld his confidence from those who practiced it. A man cast in such a mould is likely to be unpopular with that large class of persons who regard truth with less reverence; who stretch it or contract it to suit circumstances; who, in the bad sense of the phrase, are ready to become "all things to all men." They are prejudiced, obstinate, bigoted, sectarian. But there is a better and truer explanation of all this. There is a deep and heartfelt reverence for the truth as such, which, on all occasions, and every where, forbids its compromise on the ground of mere worldly expediency. There is an inner reverence for it, in kind and degree, like unto that which is felt for God himself. This was conspicuous through the whole long life of Dr. Green; and often have I heard him censuring, with far greater severity, what he considered the crooked policy of his friends, who always acted with him, than that of his opponents, who always pursued a different policy from his. His firmness was at an equal remove from fickleness and obstinacy, which are alike alien to a truly noble character. The one is barren of good as the yielding wave, the other as the unyielding rock. Although holding his opinions strongly, he was ever willing to yield them for good reasons. A fool never changes his opinions, but a wise man always will for sufficient cause.

3. He was a most fervent and instructive preacher.

Although I never heard him preach until he had passed the meridian of life; until, fearful of attacks of vertigo, to which he was subject, he generally declined the pulpit; yet the few sermons I have heard him deliver very deeply impressed his hearers, and very obviously indicated that, in the prime of his years, he was a man of no ordinary power. His utterance was distinct, his manner was calm and dignified; if he never rose to the higher style of action, he always attained its end, attention and impression; he made you feel that he entirely believed every word he uttered, and that it was of infinite moment that you should believe them also. The minister that uniformly makes this impression must be one of great power.

Nor was the impression which he made simply that of manner; his matter was always weighty, well arranged, and instructive. If his topics were commonplace, they were always important; if his discussions were sometimes dry, they were clear as a sunbeam; if you could not always adopt his opinions, there was no mistake as to what he meant. In all my intercourse with him, I had never cause to ask, "What do you mean, sir?" nor do I remember a sentence in all his writings which is not entirely transparent.

His most valuable lectures on the Shorter Catechism, and his published sermons, give a fair specimen of his ordinary style of preaching. If they have not the amplitude of Chalmers, nor the polished eloquence of Hall, nor the warmth of Davies, they have the purity of Blair, in union with a natural simplicity, which strongly fix their truly evangelical sentiments in the mind and heart. Hence the devoted attachment, both to him and his sentiments, of all who ever enjoyed his ministrations.

He greatly excelled as an expounder of the word of God. Of his talent in this way I had an abundance of opportunity of forming a judgment. The Sabbath-school teachers of Philadelphia adopted a rule to have the same Bible lesson taught on the same Sabbath in all schools of the city, and to have the lesson expounded to them by some clergyman. The lecture-room in Cherry Street was the place, and Dr. Green was the man selected. On each evening the large room was crowded by one of the most interesting and interested audiences I ever beheld; and although Dr. Green was then approaching his threescore years and ten, never did I hear more clear, and full, and fresh, and pleasing expositions of divine truth. At the close of the lecture, opportunity was given for the asking of any questions upon any points that were left unexplained, which were always answered with a promptness which showed the remarkable fullness of his mind upon all topics connected with the exposition or elucidation of the Scriptures. I know not that I ever attended a more instructive religious service. I have learned that it was greatly blessed of God to the conversion and edification of Sabbath-school teachers. He served his generation in more dignified stations, but probably in none more usefully than when expounding the word of life to nearly a thousand young men and women, who, on each successive Sabbath, sought to impress those views received from him on the minds of ten thousand children. Might not this plan be successfully revived in all our cities?

4. He was a truly devotional man. His public devotional services were always peculiarly impressive. They were solemn, pathetic, reverential, appropriate, and never unduly protracted. In the family he always commenced morning and evening prayer with imploring a blessing upon the service; and while engaged in them, all felt that he was conversing with God as a man converses with a friend. I have often heard him express his regrets at the little preparation ministers often make for conducting the devotional exercises of a congregation, and I have heard him state that in the early part of his ministry he was in the habit of writing prayers with equal regularity as sermons; and, while he never read them, nor committed them to memory, the writing of them furnished him with topics for prayer, and gave to those topics arrangement, and to the expression of them variety and appropriateness. For this thought he may have been indebted to his venerated tutor, Dr. Witherspoon, who always recommended devotional composition to his theological students, of whom Dr. Green was one.

My first sermon was preached in the Third Presbyterian Church, Philadelphia, then under the pastoral care of the Rev. Dr. Ely, and from the text "Compel them to come in." Dr. Ely was absent, and to my confusion, Dr. Green entered the church just at the opening of the service. Feeling it better to have him behind me than before me, I sent for him to the pulpit. In my ardor to stimulate ministers and Christians to do their duty, I omitted almost any allusion to the necessary agency of the Spirit to secure their success. He made the concluding prayer, in which, with his accustomed felicity, he converted the topics discussed into supplications, and then brought out most prominently and emphatically the essential truth by me omitted. I felt that the whole congregation saw and felt the defect of my sermon. His kindness was marked at the close of the service. I went to my study, re-wrote my sermon, put into it the prayer of Dr. Green, and it is unnecessary to say that it was greatly improved by the addition. I subsequently mentioned the fact to him, and we had over it a hearty laugh.

My very last interview with him impressed me with the depth of that spirit of devotion which characterized his life. He was feeble, and forgetful, and in a mood to talk but very little to any body. Hearing that I was in the city, he sent for me, that I might attend to a matter of business for him connected with the New Jersey Historical Society. I entered his study on a May morning about nine o'clock. His Greek Testament was open before him. He requested me to be seated. The business ended, he waved his hand, saying, "My devotional reading is not yet concluded; I shall be happy to see you at another time;" and as I closed the door of his study, the prayer, "God bless you," fell upon my ear; the last words I ever heard him utter. All testify that the closing years of his life were marked by a spirit remarkably devotional.

5. He possessed a truly catholic spirit. This assertion, perhaps, will startle some who only knew his pub-

lic character, and who have only heard of him as an impersonation of Old-school Presbyterianism. Yet it is true to the letter. His own views he held strongly, but in perfect charity to those who differed from him. Although his contributions and exertions were mainly confined to the organization of his own Church, it was out of consistency with himself, and not out of illiberality to others. More than once have I heard him detail an account of a visit made by the venerable Dr. Woods, for so many years the ornament of the Andover Theological Seminary. They compared views on theological and other subjects, and while they differed a little in the explanations of some positions, they radically agreed. "Would to God," I have heard him say, "that all our ministers and churches held the sentiments of my brother Woods." And after the disruption of our Church, he never permitted a day to pass without the most fervent prayers to God on the behalf of the brethren to whom he was regarded as being so violently opposed. He had none of the narrow sectarianism that would confine the Church visible to those only who walked with him; and often have I heard him rejoice in the good that was doing by Methodists, Baptists, Episcopalians, to all of whom, as Christians and as ministers, he could extend the right hand of fellowship, although on all suitable occasions he could strongly maintain the positions on which he differed from them. There is not probably a national society for the spread of the Gospel in this land to which he was not a contributor, and of which he was not a member or a manager; while he may be considered the father of nearly all the Boards and Societies of his own deeply-venerated Church. "Nobody will question the Presbyterianism of Dr. Green," said an eloquent divine, during a debate in the General Assembly, "as he was dyed in the wool." "The brother mistakes," said Dr. Green, with that promptness of repartee which he possessed; "the Lord, by his grace, made me a Presbyterian." And although the principles of his Church were interwoven with his spiritual life, and formed a part of it, yet he had the most cordial love for the children of God, by whatever name called. Never have I heard him speak with more affection of any man than of his friend, the amiable and venerated Bishop White.

6. He was remarkably gifted as a son of consolation to desponding souls. This, perhaps, was mainly owing to his own simple views of divine truth, and his rich experience of its power. He had the power of simplifying every subject on which he spoke or wrote, and of doing it in a few words. This is very apparent in his lectures on the Shorter Catechism, prepared for the youth of his own congregation. When anxious or desponding souls applied to him for direction, he first sought out the cause of trouble, and then, like a well-instructed scribe, he so simply presented and applied the remedial truth, as to give, if not immediate, yet speedy relief. He acted upon the principle, that "if the truth makes us free, we are free indeed." Hence aged, desponding Christians, and individuals asking what they should do to be saved, and from different congregations in the city, were often found in his study seeking his counsels. On such occasions there was a

kindness and blandness in his manner, which formed the greatest psssible contrast with his stern and unflinching position when contending for principles on the floor of the General Assembly.

A case in illustration of this I will state. Twenty-five years ago, the name of Miss Linnard, whose memoir has since been published, was familiar to the pious female circles of Philadelphia. She shone conspicuously among them for her fine sense, great activity, and deep piety. A minister, still living, preached a preparatory lecture in the church in Spruce Street, of which she was a member, on the text, "Lovest thou me?" which cast her into the deepest gloom. Such were the strong and vivid representations which he made as to the necessary preparations for the right partaking of the Lord's Supper, that, conscious of not possessing them, she resolved not to commune. Her sense of duty and her deep depression of feeling came into conflict, and greatly excited her soul. In this state she had recourse to Dr. Green, who had heard the lecture. "My dear child," said he, "our excellent brother seemed to forget that the Lord's table is spread, not for angels, but for sinners. He has come, not to call the righteous, but sinners to repentance. It is the weary and heavy laden he invites to himself, and to the privileges of his house." It was enough. She left his study rejoicing in the Lord; and a more joyful communion season she had never spent on earth. I heard the lecture, and the incident here narrated I have had from both parties. And this, I feel persuaded, is a fair illustration of his skill and success as a comforter of the Lord's people, and as a director of the inquiring to the cross of Jesus Christ.

It remains for me only to speak of him as a literary man. As his life and writings will do his memory full justice upon this subject, I need say but little upon it. His academic habits he carried with him into his pastoral life, and always took rank in the very first class of the educated men of his own age—with such men as Dwight, and Smith, and Wilson, and Mason. If he was excelled in brilliancy by these, and others with whom he ranked, he was fully their equal in all solid attainments. It was no ordinary tribute to his literary character that he should be selected to succeed Dr. Smith as the President of Princeton College, in which position he discharged his duties as instructor with distinguished ability, and, in a religious point of view, with distinguished usefulness. It was during his presidency that the revival occurred which, under God, brought into the Church and into the ministry such men as Dr. John Breckinridge, Dr. Hodge, Bishops McIlvaine of Ohio, and Johns of Virginia. On retiring from the presidency, he commenced the Christian Advocate, which he edited for twelve years, and whose twelve volumes give the most ample testimony to his rich scholarship, his keen discrimination, his metaphysical acumen, his sharpness as a critic, and to the extent and variety of his reading. Some of the ablest productions of his pen were written after he had passed his fourscore years; and to the very close of his life his Greek Testament was his daily study, and he could repeat passages from the Greek and Roman classics with the interest and vigor of a school boy. His habits of study he never surrendered to the last; and I have in my possession a note written to me on business in his eighty-fifth year—written with as clear, bold, and steady a hand as if written in his fortieth year. In this respect he is an example worthy of imitation by all literary men in advanced years, to study, write, and work to the last. Still waters soon stagnate; running waters never. The mind, unemployed, like the blade of Hudibras,

> "Which ate into itself, for lack
> Of somebody to hew and hack,"

preys upon itself, and soon passes away.

Such is my estimate of the character of Dr. Green. By others who knew him much longer and more intimately, it might be sketched more strongly and truly; but such are the impressions he has left upon my mind and heart by an acquaintance with him of twenty years. On the whole, I esteem him as among the ripest scholars, the most able divines, the most useful men which our country has produced. His name will be more closely connected with the history and progress of the Presbyterian Church one hundred years hence, than that of any of his predecessors. He well deserves a name and a place among "The Lights of the American Pulpit."

BEDINI, THE PAPAL NUNCIO, GONE!

And is it so, that Monsieur Archbishop Gaetano Bedini, with all his suffixes and affixes, is gone? Yes, he is gone! or, as a Hebrew of olden time would express it, "He has turned his back—he has run away." His modesty led him to avoid all public demonstrations, and he sought to get out of the country between two nights; and now he is safely, as we trust, on his way to the foot of the Holy Father, to render an account of his mission as Nuncio to Brazil, taking the United States on his way! And now that the farce is ended, and that Bedini has run away, it may be well to ponder a few matters and things concerning the man and his mission.

He came here with the high-sounding title of Archbishop of Thebes, an old city in ruins on the banks of the Nile, which it is presumed he has never seen, and never will. The Pope knows the influence of titles over weak minds, and when he wants an agent, he seeks a man fitted for the duty, and bestows upon him some high-sounding title, at once to gratify his vanity, and to gain for him credit and access among the people to whom he is sent. Bedini is sent here, as he was once sent to Bologna, as a spy; and that he might the better and the more readily perform his duties, he was made Archbishop of Thebes, and had bestowed upon him a little fillet made from the wool of holy sheep by the withered nuns of St. Agnes! Had he come simply as a priest, he would pass unnoticed; but as the Archbishop of Thebes, he rides in the mayor's carriage, and sails in a government steamer, and flourishes his canonicals at Albany and Washington! And yet some foolish people say a name is nothing!

But he merely took the United States on his way as Nuncio to Brazil! Another piece of low trickery; if not, why did he not go to Brazil? A nuncio is an embassador from the Pope to an emperor or king; when an envoy is sent to smaller states, and with limited powers, he is called an Internuncio. And that he might loom up the more largely in our republican country, the title of Nuncio to Brazil is superadded to that of Archbishop of Thebes! And the facts in the case are, that he was made archbishop of a city that he has probably never seen, and never will; and that he was commissioned as nuncio to a country upon which he has turned his back; and all for the purpose of exciting our veneration for a man, the object of whose mission is yet concealed, and whose person and character, his own noble countrymen being witnesses, are only worthy of abhorrence.

And who is the man on whom the Holy Father bestowed these titles for sinister purposes? The Italians that know him and his history being witnesses, he is a man of low origin, who acted as spy at Bologna to mark the friends of liberty, and who, when clothed with power there, because of the ferocity of his nature, gave up to death the most cruel and summary the persons that he had previously marked as a spy! He was first the spy, and next the butcher of Bologna; and then, when quailing before the indignant scorn of the civilized world, he sought to cast his crime upon Austrian soldiers, as if blood enough were not crying to heaven against them! How rarely do we find such a compound of the dregs of humanity labeled with such high-sounding titles! Spy, priest, butcher, coward, Archbishop of Thebes, and Nuncio of the Pope to the empire of Brazil, taking the United States in his way!!

And what is the moral character of this man? To those who know them, it is enough to say that he is an Italian priest with the morals of his order; and to those who know not the lives of the priests in Italy, we give in evidence the testimony of his own countrymen, who say that he was once sent to Brazil as internuncio, but was recalled because of his shameless dissoluteness. And this is the man who has been consecrating papal bishops and churches among us, and blessing the poor people, as if such bloody and unclean hands could be employed to dispense the grace and favors of God.

But he came with a letter from the Pope to our President, to congratulate him on his accession to the presidency, and asking him for his protection of our papal citizens; and with a letter from Antonelli, cardinal secretary of state, to introduce him, and praise him, and to ask kind official recognition of him! Did not the Pope know that all men were here equal before the law, civilly and religiously? If he did, what more could he ask? If he did not, how dare he to ask from us for his believers what he withholds from our people who believe the Bible? He shuts the English out of Rome, and confines them, in their worship, to a barn of a place without the walls; he drives the Americans, in their worship, under the flag of their country and to the rooms of our legation; and one of his low, vulgar dupes here says that our minister there, if found successful in converting any Romans, would be kicked out of the city; and yet he asks our President for his kind protection of his religious vassals!! And Antonelli! Mr. Cass, the Nestor of the Senate, might know all about him, and might have known more about Bedini before his recent speech in reference to him. There is not in Italy a more cold, brutal, heartless tyrant than Antonelli; there is not in Rome a more debauched clerical libertine, if the Romans speak the truth. And the man who put down the Roman Republic with French bayonets, and the man who at this hour is using all the power of the papal Church to extinguish every spark of liberty in Europe, and who is sending every Italian patriot on whom he can lay his hands to death, dungeons, or banishment, commissions the butcher of Bologna to visit our country on his way to Brazil, to congratulate our President on his accession to the chief magistracy, and to solicit his protection of our Roman Catholic fellow-citizens! What a trio of priestly tyrants, with their feet upon the neck and their daggers at the heart of liberty in Europe, and seeking liberty for their people here, where all are at liberty to worship as they will! What unblushing effrontery! Need we wonder that the Germans and Italians are excited?

But what was Bedini's errand here? Why call him here from the care of the Thebans? There must be some pressing necessity. Why send him round here on his way to Brazil? Antonelli may be able to tell, so may Bishop Hughes. We are left to conjecture. There was some little difficulty about church property in Buffalo; the same difficulty exists in other places. It is very hard to enforce the canon law here. The people here, either by contagion or absorption, imbibe some notions as to their rights and privileges which priests and bishops find it difficult to manage. Then our school laws are papistically wrong; and multitudes of papists, young and old, are forsaking the priest, and Mary, and the altar, for the Bible, the Savior, and the pulpit. It was thought that a nuncio might set these and other things all right. And Bishop Hughes himself is not regarded as the sharpest and wisest at headquarters; in Rome he is called a blundering Irishman. One was selected who had learned the trade of a spy in Italy, and who was thought to be able to spy out the true causes of the crumbling of Romanism here, and the true remedies to prevent it. But his wand would not work. He lifted it up, and called for the darkness, but it would not come; and before he got half through, God gave a tongue to the blood of Ugo Bassi, and of the other martyrs of Bologna, which proclaimed the character of Bedini through the land; and from that moment the lock of his strength was cut, and the heart of the people swelled with detestation of the monster; and the mobs, composed mostly of those from papal countries, and who felt the iron of tyranny in their souls, in Cincinnati, Baltimore, and other places, like the spittings of the volcano, only revealed the slumbering fires that lay beneath.

And the man who was toasted in New York—who rode in the mayor's carriage—who was feasted at the governor's table—who was paraded in the saloons of secretaries at Washington, had to pack his vestments in a bag—to cover his skull with something that concealed his tonsure—to steal away to Staten Island, and to pass from the deck of a tug to that of a steamer for England, to avoid the hootings of the multitudes whom the tyranny of papal Europe has driven from their homes to our shores! Did ever any man so go up as an eagle, and so come down as a goose!

And where is Bishop Hughes at the closing scene, who figured so largely in the farce when the curtain first rose? The fox, he saw the storm coming—he very likely thought Bedini a spy upon himself, as he no doubt was—he laid his hand on his side, and gave a few coughs, and found it necessary to go to Cuba for his health! Halifax would not do in mid-winter.

We only want another nuncio on his way to Brazil to complete the ruin of popery in this land, which Bedini has so largely promoted. The prestige of popery is all gone; its doctrines, its deceivings, its cunning craft, the character of its priests, taken as a clan, the most heartless impostors on earth, are all understood. The system is in a state of dissolution every where, and were it not for the alliance there is between it and despotism to support one another, it would fall to pieces at once. If the free votes of the Romans could be taken at this hour, they would vote the Pope, his cardinals, bishops, and all the inferior clergy, at least to Purgatory, if not a little beyond it.

And it is fondly to be hoped that our political men will soon be made to feel that to court the vote of the Romish priest and his people is to forfeit the vote of the Protestant.

We have seen the first and the last nuncio from Rome in the United States on his way to Brazil.

BEDINI AND DR. DUFF—A CONTRAST.

Who has not heard of Bedini, the Archbishop of Thebes—the Nuncio of the Pope to Brazil, taking the United States on his way—the spy and butcher of Bologna—the Great Runaway! He came here a bad man, on a worse mission—a low creature, though a high ecclesiastic—with nothing to recommend him but his titles and his feathers. In private, he was doing the work of him that sent him, the Pope; in public, he was courting the dignitaries of the state and the attention of the people. Scared by some demonstrations made by his own countrymen and other foreigners to testify their appreciation of his character, he passed incog. from Washington to New York. It is said that he was concealed some days in the city; but, as the storm was thickening instead of passing away, he sent for the mayor, and implored his protection. It is said that, moved by his awful terror and dread of assassination, the mayor applied to the collector for a vessel from the revenue service to carry him out of the city, but that the collector declined to interfere. It is said that application was made to the government for instructions in reference to the Latin priest, and that orders were sent to get him away as soon as possible, and at public expense. It is known that he went incog. to Staten Island; that on the day of the sailing of the Atlantic he was sent on board an old tug, the most unpretending that could be found, in order to avoid suspicion and expense, and placed on board the steamer; and that he took his departure as Nuncio from the United States to Rome, taking England on his way. Alas, poor Yorick!

If all this does not teach the Pope, and his priests, and their dupes a lesson as to the state of American feeling, and the sentiment of its free people on the subject of Popery, it is difficult to tell what can. It especially teaches them that no man, in whose skirts or on whose hands can be found a spot made by the blood of freemen, slaughtered because of even unwise efforts to obtain liberty, need expect to be otherwise treated than as a foe to humanity by the free people of this land. If the Austrian Haynau could not live in England, how could the Italian Bedini hope to enjoy an ovation in the United States? But he hoped his embroidered vestment, and his pallium, made from "the wool of holy sheep," would screen him. But no; while in no country on earth are the true ministers of religion more respected than with us, in no country on earth are priestly hypocrites more detested. Hence, after his character became known, poor Bedini had to cover his tonsure, and to hide his long coat, and to put the crucifix that dangled on his breast in his pocket, and to put aside all his priestly regalia, lest they should attract attention to his person; and then to steal away as a thief from a country where he expected to be honored as a prince. And you might as well attempt to quell the swellings of the ocean as attempt to prevent the rising of all free hearts against such a man. This the mayor of Cincinnati has learned to his cost. But he is gone! We shall be glad to learn his reception at the court of Brazil, now that he has taken the United States on his way.

As the steamer that was conveying Bedini from our shores was receding, another steamer might be seen approaching them, with a very different man on board. That man was Alexander Duff. His history is a brief but pregnant one. In his youth he devoted himself to God and the cause of Missions. He left Scotland, his native land, for India in 1829, and was wrecked on the rocks of the Cape of Good Hope, losing every thing but his Bible, which was found on the beach where it was washed by the waves. Nothing daunted, he sailed thence for India, and in a fierce hurricane, peculiar to those latitndes, was again wrecked at the mouth of the Ganges, and only escaped with his life. He reached Calcutta, with his plans all formed, and with the fixed resolution to carry them out. If esteemed a fanatic at home, when Moderatism, like a mountain of ice, crushed and chilled the heart of the Church of Scotland, he was received with marked coldness by officials abroad. One man only encouraged him, and he was a heathen, the famous Ramohun Roy. The young missionary hired a small room, and commenced his great work with five heathen boys. Such was the small beginning of the Church of Scotland's Missions in India! That room grew into the famous College of Calcutta, now the light of India, and the five boys into fourteen hundred pupils.

On the disruption of the Church of Scotland, the missionary decided to go out with the Free Church; and although the college buildings were mainly erected through his own individual exertions, he was compelled to abandon them, to go out empty-handed, and to find accommodations as he could for his pupils. But when Christ's crown and headship in the Church were at stake, he could not hesitate a moment; and although not so well accommodated as formerly, that college was never so useful or more fully attended than now. The great and successful labors of this missionary in Calcutta are felt in all India, from Ceylon to the Himalayas; they are felt in their reflex influence on the entire Church of God. His great mental power, his entire consecration, his sleepless industry, his wise plans, his perseverance in following them out, have enabled him to do in India a work of vast magnitude, and of the greatest importance; and although under fifty years of age, his name is in all the earth as "the Apostle of India."

On the death, we might almost say the translation of Dr. Chalmers, this missionary was selected to fill his place as a professor of divinity in the Free Church College, as the man best fitted to succeed to the chair vacated by him who in his life was designated as "the greatest of living Scotchmen." But he declined the honor, for the reason that he had consecrated himself to the heathen, and desired to live and die among them. On his return to Scotland he was elected, by acclamation, moderator of the Free Assembly of 1851. Since that time, although in feeble health, he has been through Scotland, England, and Ireland, in labors abundant, and with a fervid eloquence that has not been surpassed, seeking to rouse every branch of the Church of God to more earnest efforts for the conversion of the world. The writer of this article heard him, on one occasion, pour forth his soul for three hours upon the most densely crowded and deeply interested audience he ever saw; his appeals now melting the entire assembly into tears, and now filling the ample building with thundering applause.

This great missionary, the Rev. Alexander Duff, is now in our country. He was landed on our shores just as Bedini had left them. He brought with him no letters from pope, prince, or prelate. The fame of his labors and Christian virtues had preceded him. No Antonelli lauds his gifts and his virtues. He needs no such doubtful praise. He is no archbishop of tottering pillars, and crumbling walls, and piles of ruins, amid which the cormorant and the bittern, the owl and the raven hoot, and over which the adder and the serpent trail their slime. He comes not here on his way as a messenger from a doting tyrant in the Old World to some other tyrant in the New. His hair is unshaven on his head. He wears no priestly vestments to catch vulgar eyes. He is simply a missionary who has spent most of his life among the heathen, and who has come to tell us of the degradation, and the wants, and the rising civilization of India. He is simply a noble, self-sacrificing Christian minister, who has come with the greetings of Protestant Britain to Protestant America. Although a Scotchman by birth, we all claim him as a fellow-citizen; although a Presbyterian in religion, we all claim him as a fellow-Christian.

His life and labors are known to the world. He has worn himself out in seeking to excite, not to suppress free thought—to elevate, not to depress the race; in seeking to teach the world that faith in Christ, not faith in the Pope, is the way to heaven. No blood cries to heaven against him. No Scotchman will rise up save to claim him as a countryman, and to proclaim him "every inch a man." As he passes through the land, no mobs will meet him with effigies; no police will be needed to protect him; and if he rides not in the mayor's carriage—if he sails not in a government steamer—if he is not feasted in a governor's house—if he is not paraded in secretaries' saloons in Washington, he will be welcomed as a Christian philanthropist of the highest stamp by every Christian man from one end of the Union to the other.

And when his journeyings are ended, and the time for his return to his own land has arrived, he will need no protection from mayor or magistrate—he will need no tug to draw him from his concealment to a steamer in the bay, to avoid the hootings of the multitudes that would greet him if he went on board at the wharf. We will accompany him to the ship; we will give him our parting blessing, and receive his; and we will sorrow most of all that we shall see his face no more.

BEDINI AND DUFF—ANOTHER CONTRAST.

WITHIN a few months past our country has been visited by two persons, each celebrated in his way, and creating no little excitement, and each the representative of systems and principles as diverse as the noon of night and the noon of day. The one was the celebrated Monsieur Gaetano Bedini, Archbishop of Thebes, Apostolic Nuncio to Brazil, taking the United States on his way, and so forth, and so forth. He came with high-sounding titles; with letters from the Pope, and his secretary, Antonelli, lauding his talents and his virtues; dressed in full regalia, as brilliant as the plumage of the strutting peacock. These things took for a time with that stratum of humanity with which such things take, and the creature, thus dressed up in names and in vestments, was paraded here and there as quite a character. And such he certainly was—and is, if he yet survives his fright on leaving our shores. The passage of this magnificent ecclesiastic through portions of our country is yet familiar to all our people. To make political capital with those who regard the character and blessings of such a harlequin, politicians, here and there, treated him with some external marks of respect. But when his true character was made known by those Italians who sought here an asylum from papal cruelty; when the cry of the blood of the murdered Ugo Bassi, and of those who fell with him as martyrs to liberty in Bologna, proclaimed from the Atlantic to the Pacific that Bedini was their executioner, it was all over with the tonsured nuncio. The storm commenced on the banks of the Ohio; it followed him across the Alleghanies to Washington, Baltimore, and New York. Finding that the "Veneratissimo" John, of New York, had retired from the track of the storm to Cuba, under plea of health, he concealed himself as he could, in secluded parts of the city, until the plan of his hegira was completed. A day or two previous to the sailing of a steamer for England, a few men, muffled, and looking suspiciously around, might be seen crossing to Staten Island, where they were hidden away by some friend, as were the spies of Joshua in Jericho by Rahab. On the morning of the sailing of the steamer, an old "tug" might be seen pressing its way to an adjacent wharf. As it put forth no pretensions to be a boat for passengers, no decent person thought of noticing it. As the noble steamer fired her signal guns for departure, the muffled gentry made their way to the tug, which swung from her moorings as soon as they stepped on board. She paddled into the stream; Bedini was smuggled on board the steamer; and thus he passed away from our shores amid appalling fears and terrors, which made the little hair left by the priestly razor on his head to stiffen into straight lines, and without a solitary being to bid him farewell. We take it for granted that his priestly attendants were rejoiced to get rid of him.

It is said that when he got fairly on board, he commenced most devoutly kissing a crucifix; and that when he got quietly seated, he read his Missal with race-horse rapidity. When, during the voyage, the winds of February rolled up the waves of the Atlantic into stormy billows, it is said he manifested great terror; and, when he got safely to London, he wrote back for our edification the famous letter of February 17th, to the Archbishop of Baltimore, in which he seems to weep with rage, to pray like Lucifer, to laugh like a hyena, to deny alleged charges so as to prove them, and which, after gravely informing us that he sent "a number of pictures of the Blessed Virgin of Rimini," "the portentous moving of whose pupils" has rendered it "a picture so blessed and so full of celestial inspiration," he offers the following prayer to "the blessed Lady of Rimini:" "O may this most powerful mother of the God-Man console with her celestial glance so many of her children who will seek in her maternal heart the fountain of so many graces, and may she in so many others also, who, bathed in the blood of her Son, still obstinately refuse to call her their mother, work not the less rare prodigy of opening their eyes." This letter should be preserved in every museum of the world as a fair specimen of the literature of the Roman priesthood—of the progress of the Italian mind—of the animus of papal ecclesiastics, and as the most wonderful sample of unadulterated balderdash which this age has produced. With this famous letter poor Bedini has disappeared from view; but whether he has gone to Thebes, or has taken some other route to Brazil, or whether he is stirring up the

Holy Father to seek redress for his "discourteous and insulting treatment," which was sufficient to cause "any nation to descend a thousand degrees in the scale of its dignity," is not known. Only one thing is certain, we shall not soon again see the like of Monsieur Archbishop Gaetano Bedini.

Such was one of the celebrated characters to whom I have above alluded. He came, and he has gone; but the telling lesson of his coming and going remain.

The other character by whom we have been visited, and who has created no small excitement, is Alexander Duff, a simple, untitled Scotchman; a devoted Presbyterian minister; for nearly a quarter of a century a most successful missionary in India; and with nothing but his own high moral character and great eloquence to arrest attention. He came on the earnest entreaty of a noble-hearted merchant,* without any blood on his hands, and simply as a Gospel minister. He came without any letters from men of high name to men in high places. He needed none. And from his first appearance in public to the last, thousands thronged to hear him, and thousands were unable to press within the sound of his voice. He had no masses to mutter; his message to all was the simple Gospel, whether spoken in the Capitol of the nation, or upon the banks of the Hudson, or the Ohio, or the St. Lawrence. He had no schemes of darkness to carry out—no earthly master to serve or to laud. He would enthrone Jesus amid the nations and in the hearts of all men; and from New York to Washington, and thence

* George H. Stuart, Esq., of Philadelphia.

by Pittsburg and Cincinnati to St. Louis, and thence by Chicago and Detroit to and through the Canadas, and by the way of Boston back again to New York, his route has been a constant ovation. Every where he was hailed at his coming and blessed at his departing by all good men.

The last week of his sojourn among us was the busy week of our religious anniversaries. Who that heard him at the Missionary Convention, before the Christian Union, the Tract and Bible Societies, before the Presbyterian or the American Board of Foreign Missions, can ever forget the thrilling eloquence and the apostolical zeal with which he urged the various tribes of Israel to go up and to possess the land. Nor were his words finely arranged for the occasion, and elegantly delivered, falling upon the audience like snow-flakes upon the running stream, and forgotten by speaker and hearer at the close of the service. They were words from the heart, which all felt, and which will never be forgotten. They were nails driven into a sure place. He there scattered seed broadcast which will bear fruit long after he has fallen to sleep on the banks of the Ganges.

The morning of his departure was one of thrilling interest. He was the guest of Robert L. Stuart, Esq., who entertained him and his friends with princely hospitality. There, surrounded by the family of his host, and a few of his more intimate friends, he led in the morning prayer—a scene never to be forgotten. After attending to a few items of business, he went with his friends to a meeting for prayer in the church of the

Rev. Mr. Thomson. The church was nearly filled with ministers and people. The services were closed by Dr. Duff in a few simple, sublime words of farewell, and with the benediction; and such was the throng to shake his hand in a responsive farewell, that with difficulty he could enter the carriage that was to convey him to the steamer. But the scene at the steamer defies description. The wharf and the noble Pacific were crowded with clergymen and Christians, assembled to bid him adieu. Many could only take him by the hand, weep, and pass on. Never did any man leave our shores so entirely encircled with Christian sympathy and affection. All felt that that was to be a final adieu, and they mourned most of all that they should see his face no more.

When ordered to the wharf from the steamer, the people sought every point where they could catch a last glimpse of him. As the noble boat slowly but majestically moved from her berth, not a word was uttered. Some held up a white handkerchief—some waved a hat; but not a word was uttered! The swelling emotions of all forbade applause or utterance. We looked as long as we could discern his countenance, and then turned away, praying to Heaven that his voyage homeward and then eastward might be as safe and prosperous as his visit here had been popular and useful. No such man has visited us since the days of Whitfield. And as, amid waving hats and handkerchiefs, and the flowing tears of many, the majestic Pacific moved out from her dock, many exclaimed, What a contrast is this with the departure of Bedini!

Dr. Duff has come and he has gone; and the telling lessons of his coming and of his going remain. And the coming and the departure of these two men, Bedini and Duff, give the true key-note to Popery and Protestantism, as they are regarded by the people of the United States. A few more Bedinis and winking Madonnas of Rimini, and Popery will be the synonym of absurdity.

THE REV. ARCHIBALD ALEXANDER, D.D.

A LETTER TO A FRIEND.

My dear Sir,—The true idea of Dr. Archibald Alexander must be ever confined to those who knew him, and who were capable of appreciating his character; and that idea, even with such, like the idea of the true or the beautiful, is more easily felt than expressed. You ask me to give you my idea of him. It is impossible for me to transfer it to paper just as it lies enshrined in my own mind; but for the sake of those who never saw or knew him, and who may desire a portrait of the man, I will make the attempt to comply with your request.

My first sight of the man and interview with him was in the month of November, 1826. My first feeling was that of disappointment. He was small of stature, rather slender in person, negligent in dress, rather reserved in company, and with a voice in conversation pitched on a higher key than ordinary, and rather inclining to a squeak. Having just passed from under the tuition of Dr. Griffin, the contrast between my past and future teacher was too great not to be felt at the moment. He placed me, however, by his kind and cordial manner, soon at ease; and as he was reading my introductions and papers, I sought, as well as I could, to read his person and countenance. I soon concluded that his broad and strongly-marked forehead, his dark and penetrating eye, his brief but comprehensive questions, his rapid conceptions, meant something; and I left his room deeply interested and impressed by the interview. On the next Sabbath, in the afternoon, I heard him, for the first time, preach in the oratory of the seminary. He spoke sitting in his chair. He read a passage of Scripture, and then, as was his manner, raising his spectacles from his eyes to his head, he commenced talking. His voice was peculiar, and his manner; his matter was simple. As he progressed, I became interested—absorbed. Although seated in the middle of the room, and in the midst of students, I thought he was preaching to me, and revealing the very secrets of my heart; and as his penetrating eye glanced from seat to seat, I instinctively shrunk behind the person that sat before me, in order to avoid his reading me through and through. That first sermon I have never forgotten. As a preacher to the conscience and to the experience of men, I have never known or read of his superior. While under his instructions, my esteem grew into respect, my respect into love, and my love into admiration of the man; and my intercourse with him in subsequent years, on more equal terms, and on a wider platform than that of a student, has left the impression on my heart, that in all the elements of true greatness the Church of Christ has had but few such ministers.

"What makes you think Dr. Alexander a great man?" said rather a captious minister to me one day.

"That is a question I never thought of," was my reply. And the question was a natural one for persons to ask who but occasionally saw him, and who heard him but occasionally preach. He was not eloquent, like Chalmers and Robert Hall; he was not learned, like Bentley and Porson; he was not polished to cold elegance, like Blair, nor into crimson gorgeousness, like Melville; nor was his a courtly polish of manner in public or in private, which often makes weak men quite impressive. In what, then, you will ask, consisted that emphatic character which so deeply impressed itself upon all who ever knew him, and, indeed, upon his age? In a rare combination of characteristics, so nicely blended as to conceal each other, and as yet to make an almost perfect whole.

He was a man, if not of various, of solid learning. To this all his students and his works testify. He was a child of nature in all his habits; in his modes of thought, in his manner of expression, in his tones of voice, in his gestures, in his keen wit, in his occasional sarcasms, in his very laugh, he was perfectly natural. It would seem as if the idea of doing a thing genteelly, or according to rule, or for effect, was never before him. This was one of the highest charms of his character. He was a man of godly sincerity. He had no concealed ends—no hidden plans to produce future results. He manifested all that he felt. In an intercourse with him, of more or less frequency, for twenty-five years, some of which was confidential, I have never known him to advocate policy. His was the most simple-hearted piety; he read the Bible like a child, and he exercised a simple faith in all it taught and promised. There was no effort to explain away its doctrines, or to modify its principles by the teachings of philosophy, falsely so called. He was a metaphysician, and yet all the metaphysics and German mysticism upon earth weighed not a feather with him against one simple text of Scripture fairly interpreted. His mind and heart were imbued with divine truth, and his experience of its power was rich and ripe. He had a sympathizing heart; no person ever resorted to him in vain for counsel or aid. He entered into your circumstances and feelings, and soon felt as you felt. Indeed, I have known his sympathies produce in him a nervous excitement, so as greatly to interrupt his comfort. He knew when to speak and when to be silent. It was in the month of January, 1842, he came to my bereaved family to bury one of our children, the second taken from us within a few days. He sat by my side without saying a word for some time; at length, breaking the silence, he uttered this memorable expression: "I have not come to comfort you, my friend; the Lord only can comfort you;" and again a long silence ensued. After the emotions excited by our first meeting subsided, the conversation became natural, and on his part instructive and greatly comforting. He was a preacher of the rarest excellence; natural, scriptural, pungent, experimental, and, at times, overwhelming in his application of truth to the saint and to the sinner. Nor had he lost any of his interest down to old age. The last address I ever heard from him was made to the Synod of New Jersey, at its meeting in Elizabethtown in 1850, and I never heard a better one, or one that more deeply interested his crowded audience. As a professor of theology, he was able, discriminating, sound in the faith, and most ardently attached to the great doctrines of grace; and as a teacher, he was as a father to his pupils. Their location, their joys and their sorrows, their failures and successes, seemed all known to him; their names seemed ever before him, and he never met them but with paternal emotions. His death was just like his life — calm, natural, collected, and pleasant. None would have it, indeed, otherwise. There was no pain of body — no anxiety of mind — no fears as to the Church. His family was all around him. The Synod of New Jersey was in session. His beloved seminary was flourishing. "My work," said he, "is done, and it is best I should go home." And he went home. And the Synod of New Jersey, and many ministers from other synods, and from distant places, carried him to his burial.

"The Lord reigneth; let the earth rejoice."

REV. SAMUEL MILLER, D.D.

LAST INTERVIEW.

Among the most polished, popular, and learned ministers that have adorned the American Church, was the Rev. Dr. Samuel Miller. In stature of the medium size, formed with remarkable symmetry, with mild blue eye, bald head, high forehead, and a countenance remarkably bland and prepossessing, he immediately commanded the respect of all with whom he came in contact. His politeness was such as to gain for him the American sobriquet of the American Chesterfield; his affability was such as to attract even the fondling attention of children; so ready was he in conversation, and so full of anecdote, as to make him the attractive centre of every circle which he graced with his presence; and so wise and prudent was he withal, that his advice and counsels were sought by his brethren and by the churches as if he were an oracle. In his youth he was greatly popular as a preacher, and down to the close of his long life was remarkably solemn and instructive. Thoroughly evangelical and devotedly pious, his ministrations were sought beyond those of almost any of his contemporaries. He was a man of varied learning, of retentive memory; was a graceful, easy, and polished writer, and, to as great an extent as almost any man of his day, enjoyed both an American and European reputation. He was a voluminous author, an able controvertist, a fine ecclesiastical historian, and an able and beloved professor in the Theological Seminary at Princeton, from its foundation to the close of his long and brilliant life. Dignified without haughtiness, condescending without descending, affable without garrulity, polite without the cold correctness which chills, firm in his opinions without bigotry, catholic without any approach to latitudinarianism, and remarkably generous in all his sympathies, he made even his enemies to be at peace with him, and embalmed his memory in the hearts of all good men; and the hundreds of students that enjoyed his instructions as a professor, while they reverenced him as a teacher, loved him as a father.

The Historical Society of New Jersey met at Princeton, now a place of patriotic, and classic, and sacred associations. It was a noble gathering of men distinguished in their various professions as jurists, advocates, professors, and divines; and there was a most cordial greeting and commingling of these historic associates. All differences in sentiments, professions, and politics were laid aside while in the pursuit of the one common object of honoring New Jersey by collecting materials for its history, and to rescue from oblivion the names of her many heroic and distinguished sons.

But one was absent who had rarely been absent before, and who was one of the founders and vice-presidents of the society; one whose bland and polished manners always attracted regard, and whose venerable aspect always deeply impressed. His absence from the meeting, and in the town of his residence, excited inquiry; and when it was announced that Dr. Miller was very seriously sick, there was in the meeting a deep expression of sorrow and sympathy. It was solemnly felt by all that in those historic gatherings we should see his face no more.

His son conveyed to me a message from his father that he would like to see me on the morning of the next day, if convenient. The hour of our interview was fixed; and, as other engagements required punctuality, I was there at the moment.

But, as the barber had just entered the room, he was not quite ready to see me, and he sent requesting me to wait half an hour. This my other engagements absolutely forbade; and on sending him word to that effect, he invited me to his room. As I entered it, the picture which presented itself was truly impressive. The room was his library, where he had often counseled, cheered, and instructed me. There, bolstered in a chair, feeble, wan, and haggard, was my former teacher and friend, one half of his face shaven, with the soap on the other half, and the barber standing behind his chair. The old sweet smile of welcome played upon his face, and having received his kind hand and greetings, he requested me to take a seat by his side. His message was a brief one; he had written a history of the Theological Seminary for the Historical Society which was not yet printed, and he wished an unimportant error into which he thought he had fallen to be corrected; and that there might be no mistake, he wished me to write it down, thus showing his ruling passion for even verbal accuracy. When his object in sending for me was gained, he then, in a most composed and intensely solemn manner, thus addressed me:

"My dear brother, my sands are almost run, and this will be, probably, our last interview on earth. Our intercourse, as professor and pupil, and as ministers, has been one of undiminished affection and confidence. I am just finishing my course; and my only regrets are that I have not served my precious Master more fervently, sincerely, and constantly. Were I to live my life over again, I would seek more than I have done to know nothing but Christ. The burdens that some of us have borne in the Church will now devolve upon you and your brethren; see to it that you bear them better than we have done, and with far greater consecration; and as this will, no doubt, be our last interview here, it will be well to close it with prayer. As I am too feeble to kneel, you will excuse me if I keep my chair."

I drew my chair before him, and knelt at his feet. The colored barber laid aside his razor and brush, and knelt by his side. As he did not indicate which of us was to lead in prayer, I inferred, because of his feebleness, that it would be right for me to do so; and while seeking to compose my own mind and feelings to the effort, I was relieved by hearing his own sweet, feeble, melting accents. His prayer was brief, but unutterably touching and impressive. He commenced it by thanksgiving to God for his great mercy in calling us into the fellowship of the saints, and then calling us into the ministry of his Son. He then gave thanks that we ever sustained to one another the relation of pupil and teacher, and for our subsequent pleasant intercourse as ministers of the Gospel. He thanked God for the many years through which he permitted him to live, and for any good which he enabled him to do. "And now, Lord," said he, "seeing that thine aged, imperfect servant is about being gathered to his fathers, let his mantle fall upon thy young servant, and for more of the Spirit of Christ than he has ever enjoyed. Let the years of thy servant be as the years of his dying teacher; let his ministry be more devoted, more holy, more useful; and when he comes to die, may he have fewer regrets to make in reference to his closing ministrations. We are to meet no more on earth; but when thy servant shall follow his aged father to the grave, may we meet in heaven, there to sit, and shine, and sing with those who have turned many to righteousness, who have washed their robes and made them white in the blood of the Lamb. Amen."

I arose from my knees, melted as is wax before the fire. My full heart sealed my lips. Through my flowing tears I took my last look of my beloved teacher, the counselor of my early ministry, the friend of my ripening years, and one of the most lovely and loved ministers with which God has ever blessed the Church. Every thing impressed me: the library, his position, the barber; his visage, once full and fresh, now sallow and sunken; his great feebleness, his faithfulness, his address, and, above all, that prayer, never, never to be forgotten! He extended his emaciated hand from under the white cloth that draped from his breast to his knees, and, taking mine, gave me his parting, his last benediction. That address—that prayer—that blessing, have made enduring impressions. It was the most solemn and instructive last interview of my life.

When I next saw him he was sleeping in his coffin in the front parlor of his house, where he often, with distinguished urbanity and hospitality, entertained, instructed, and delighted his friends. That parlor was crowded by distinguished strangers, and by many of his former pupils, who mourned for him as for a father—for a father he was to them all. And as they passed around to take a parting sight of his countenance, from which even death could not remove its accustomed placid, benevolent smile, their every bosom heaved with intense emotion, their eyes were suffused with tears; and could every tongue utter the emotions of their hearts, it would be in the language of Elisha when he gazed on Elijah ascending before him unto heaven, "My father, my father, the chariot of Israel, and the horsemen thereof."

His death was as calm and triumphant as his life was pure, disinterested, and lovely; and as pious men carried him to his burial, and as we covered up his remains under the clods of the valley, the prayer arose at least from one heart, "May I live the life of this righteous man, and let my last end be like his."

There are many scenes in the life of Dr. Miller that memory frequently recalls—scenes in the class-room, in the General Assembly, in the Synod of New Jersey, in the pulpit, in the social party—scenes which occurred during the conflicts of parties, and in the frank and unrestrained intercourse of social life. In them all Dr. Miller was pre-eminently like himself. But the scene by which I most love to recall him, and which memory most frequently recalls, is that parting scene in his study. Oh, may that parting prayer be answered !*

* Written for a forthcoming work of the Rev. Dr. Sprague.

AN ELDER INDEED.

A KIND, intelligent, firm, pious, peace-making, prayerful man is a great blessing to a church. Even when in a low social position, he grows into great influence; but when in the position to which education and wealth can elevate, he becomes a pillar in the Church, and his influence is felt for good on all its members and interests. To a young pastor he is a gift of God. With such a man as a counselor and friend, the minister who is just putting on the harness will be safely guided through many difficult cases; his fiery zeal will be repressed—his errors will be excused—his hours of despondency will be cheered by kind interferences—he will be comforted amid the discouragements which are often so trying to the faith of the youthful embassador for Christ. Such a man I found in the eldership of the Church of E——, who was only a comfort to me from the day of our first acquaintance until the day of his death. He was an elder worthy of double honor; and the peculiar traits of his character are worthy of being held up for universal imitation.

He was born in the year 1789, and before the community, or country, had time to recover from the effects of the war of the Revolution. Without any patrimony, he was left an orphan in his youth, both his parents dying within a few months of one another.

He was thus a child of Providence almost from his infancy. In the town of Newark, and while yet a youth, he became hopefully pious, under the ministry of the Rev. Dr. Griffin. Although nothing like levity had ever marked his conduct, he now became deeply serious and thoughtful, and sought to supply the deficiencies of his earlier education by devoting his evenings to study, reading, and religious things. When his companions, many of whom went before him to unwept graves, were out in carousal, he was at the meeting for prayer or for conference, or at home in his room, seeking to store his mind with useful knowledge. This course obtained for him the confidence of his employers, and the respect of all his companions. Early in his married life he returned to his native town, and became a member of our Church in the year 1815, and of which, for thirty-eight years, he has been a consistent and devoted member. For several years he followed his profession of daily toil. As he became known to the people, he won their confidence. He was for several years an alderman of the borough, and a justice of the peace, and a collector of the township, and deputy mayor. In the year 1831 he was elected a ruling elder, and in 1834 a deacon of the Church, in both which capacities he served until his sudden removal from the midst of us.

The leading characteristic of this man was common sense; and this went very far to supply all the defects of education. It was apparent in the formation of his opinions—in the expression of them—in his plans and arrangements—and in the utter absence of pretension, even when his influence was strongest. He weighed matters and subjects; he was cool and collected; and when his opinions were formed upon subjects which he could comprehend, there was but little need of revising or changing them; and as he usually kept within the range of such subjects, his opinions were always respected even by those who differed from him.

And while firm in his own opinions, he was remarkably tolerant of the opinions of others. It is frequently the case that men of narrow education and strong sense are very dogmatical; and when they acquire money, offensively arrogant. The very opposite was the character of our friend. He could modify his opinions for reasons; but, while he tenaciously held his own, he was tolerant of adverse opinions; and where conscience was not interfered with, when outvoted, he turned round and worked with his brethren.

While in political and civil life he mingled much with his fellow-men, he was an honest politician and an upright magistrate. He was not of those who thought the country ruined when his party did not succeed, and who, to carry their point, think all things fair. He would rather be right than successful, and in the use of honest means could bear to be defeated; and, save by those who felt themselves condemned by his integrity, or defeated by his influence, we have never heard his civil life reproached. To the extent of our knowledge, it is without spot.

It is very rarely that we see gentleness and firmness combined to the same extent as they were in his case. His tones, especially among the afflicted, were gentle as those of woman. So great was his sympathy as often to overcome him. He was pleasant and accommodating to a remarkable degree. It seemed almost impossible to excite him to passion; and what others would interpret as an insult, he would pleasantly turn off with a smile. These are usually the characteristics of a person easily decoyed from his object and turned from his purpose; but in the case of our friend, they were connected with a firmness of purpose which yielded not. You might abuse or flatter, but he was firm. Like the well-constructed arch, the heavier the pressure, the firmer he became. You might reason, or scold, or abuse, he might or might not be silent; and when you hoped you had moved him, he was only drawing reasons from your conduct for increased firmness. Such a man in this shuffling age, when men have sails to catch all winds, is as a stream of water in the desert, as the shadow of a great rock in a weary land. I always knew just where to find him. He was a true man, and as kind as true.

His sympathy for the fatherless and widow in their affliction was a leading trait of his character, and in his case seemed to be a special gift of God. How many a widow have I heard bless him; and to how many an orphan has he been a father! His own house has been the home of the orphan, and who, because of his kindness, never knew the want of a father. He did not wait to be sought for by the widow, he sought them out. He strove to infuse the comforts of religion into their desolate hearts; and, when necessary, with true liberality, to supply their temporal wants from his own purse. He had his regular rounds among these, which were seldom neglected, until the hand of disease was laid upon him. It was a part of his religion to visit the fatherless and widows in their affliction, as well as to keep himself unspotted from the world.

As an elder of the Church, but few, save his pastor, can estimate his worth. His uniform kindness, his practical wisdom, his gentleness toward the erring, his firmness when requisite, his peculiar talent as a peace-maker between brethren, his aptness in family visitation, his intelligent firmness as a Presbyterian, his thorough, though quiet opposition to all fanaticism and folly, entitled him to the double honor of those who rule well. Within the last twenty-five years the Church has been more disturbed with new doctrines and measures, with new and ephemeral modes of reformation, than for a century previous; and in reference to all this class of things, I know not of a solitary instance in which he swerved for a moment from the good old ways. We have had our own differences of opinion as to the propriety of certain measures among ourselves, but I have never known him for a moment to set up his will against those of his brethren, or to turn for a moment from the course which promised to promote the future welfare of the Church. He was just such an elder as would be a comfort to any minister, and a blessing to any Church.

But, after all, his simple, unfeigned piety was the basis of his entire character. He remembered his Creator in the days of his youth; and he grew up from the blade to the ear, and onward to the full corn in the ear. His views of truth were settled; he believed truth to practice it; he had a full conception of what a profession of Christianity required, and he sought to live accordingly. He was a man of prayer in private, in his family, in public. None could hear him pray without feeling that the secret of the Lord was with him; and never was I more affected than when, after the paralysis which unfitted him for many duties for two or three years, he said to me, "Do not call upon me to pray; I have the heart to pray, but my memory fails, and the Lord has taken away my tongue."

His religious experience was in full keeping with his life. It was free from all sudden alternations. It was never up to burning heat, nor down to the freezing point. His growth in grace was steady, and, like many living springs, very much unaffected by spiritual drought or by spiritual showers. For years that are past he possessed the comfort of the full assurance of faith; and while he mourned over his sins, he could say, "I know in whom I have believed, and that he will keep that which I have committed unto him."

When death came, it found him as a shock of corn fully ripe to be gathered into the garner. He was walking about the streets in the morning; he returned to the sick-bed of his dying wife, with whom he had a deeply solemn interview, which proved to be their last on earth; deeply affected, he went to his bed to rest, where he was seized with apoplexy before noon, and without struggle, and probably without feeling the pain of dying, a little after the setting of the evening's sun, the silver cord was loosed, and the spirit returned to the God that gave it.

> "So fades a summer cloud away,
> So sinks the gale when storms are o'er;
> So gently shuts the eye of day,
> So dies a wave along the shore."

This elder was not a great man, nor a polished man, nor a learned man. He was never ambitious of character which he did not possess. He went in and out as a plain, simple, unostentatious citizen, as he was. There was nothing in his dress, or address, or appearance, to arrest the attention of the stranger. We claim for him no perfection, nor do we hold the doctrine. But his moral principles were strong; his moral virtues were of the highest order; his piety was deep and affectionate; and attachment to the right and true was the law of his life. He was a hero in his way and place. And having filled the orbit in which he moved with light; having performed honestly and manfully the duties which were given him to do; having fought the good fight of faith for nearly fifty years without fainting or weariness, and having gone to the grave without spot or blemish upon his name, we are as willing to crown him as if he fell a general on the victorious field of battle—as if, like Adams, Calhoun, or Clay, he died in his senatorial robes. There are heroes in low places as in high, in private as in public life; and it is promotive of the moral virtues in all the ranks of life, that wherever a true hero falls, willing hands should be always found ready to bind the victor's wreath upon his brow.

MARY MAGDALENE.

THE Bible contains many brilliant narratives of the piety and of the faith of woman. If first in transgression, she has never been last in the works of faith and labor of love. Nobly has she labored under both dispensations, and in every age, to erase from the earth the traces of the curse of which she was to so great a degree the cause. In that brilliant chapter of the Epistle to the Hebrews, in which Paul so eloquently depicts the power of faith, we find the name of Sarah on the same roll with that of Enoch, Noah, and Abraham; and that of Rahab with those of Moses, and Joseph, and Joshua, and Gideon, and Samuel, and David. And may it not be that it was in a wise deference to Eastern feeling as to woman that he omits the names of Rachel, and Jochebed, and Hannah, and Esther, and Ruth, and Deborah, and Abigail, and the women of Shunem, when he crowds into such a glorious galaxy the names of so many men, whose faith was no more illustrious than theirs? Woman illustrates every page of Jewish history by her courage, fortitude, and faith.

And such also is the fact as to the New Testament history. Commencing with Mary, the mother of our Lord, what a remarkable display of faith, fidelity, and heroic devotion do we find in the females connected with the history of Christ and his apostles, and with the collecting and planting of the first churches! Every where kind and attentive to the Savior; every where sitting under his teaching; along the whole track of his public ministry seeking from him cures for their sick with characteristic earnestness; last at the cross, first at the grave; every where the helpers of the apostles in their arduous labors, the Christian Scriptures bear the most emphatic testimony to the heroism of their faith. And, perhaps, in all the Bible there is not a woman whose faith and piety shine more brightly than do those of Mary Magdalene, whose simple and beautiful history, as drawn by the "beloved disciple," we have in the 20th chapter of the Gospel of St. John.

To a brief history of this woman, and a brief statement of the lessons which it teaches, we now invite the attention of our readers.

She is called Magdalene, because she resided in the little village of Magdala, which lay on the shore of the Sea of Tiberias, where, it is said, she was a plaiter of hair for vain and wicked women. So great a sinner was she, that she is said to have been possessed by "seven devils," which were cast out by the Savior. This some interpret literally; others figuratively, as expressive of her great sinfulness and forgiveness. She was doubtless the woman who, in the house of Simon, the Pharisee, washed the feet of Jesus with her tears, and wiped them with the hair of her head. Simon thought that the admission of her to such familiarity was an evidence either that the Savior knew not her character, or that he was not sufficiently strict in his conduct. This was the occasion of the inimitable parable of the "two debtors." She was forgiven much, and she loved much. After her conversion, she attended him on his journeys, and ministered to him of her substance. She attended him on his last journey from Galilee to Jerusalem, and was a deeply-affected witness of all the scenes connected with his death. She was among the disciples who thronged the hall of the High Priest during his trial, and her heart melted, like wax before the flame, when she heard the Holy One condemned to death on perjured testimony. She followed him to the cross; and as she looked upon the dying struggle, and heard the words, "It is finished," uttered by his parched and quivering lips, and saw him bow his head and give up the ghost, her love was kindled into a flame.

The crucifixion scene is over. The tragedy of Calvary closes amid the hiding of the light of the sun, and the convulsions of nature, and the coming forth of the dead! Jesus died the just for the unjust; and while his body is taken in one direction for its burial, Mary retires in another, to prepare and mix spices and ointments for embalming it. She poured precious ointment on him while living; he is not to be forgotten now that he is dead. "Many waters can not quench love, neither can the floods drown it."

Men can not tell us what it is to love; they might as well attempt to paint a sound. It is an affection which demonstrates its own power, and the force of that demonstration is only known by those in whose bosom the affection lives. Love knows no fear; no barrier can arrest it; through floods and flames it will press its way in the pursuit of its object. And the love of woman is proverbially strong; that of Mary bore her above all fear. The sepulchre where Jesus was laid was removed at some distance from the city, and, regardless of all danger, she went forth while it was yet dark, on the first day of the week, to his grave. Alone she went through the silent streets to a spot particularly gloomy, and where even the philosophic mind is filled with fairy visions, and to a grave guarded by Roman soldiers, and that she might find in the place of the dead the body of her Lord. Finding the stone removed from the sepulchre, and the body of Jesus not there, overwhelmed with sorrow, she ran to his disciples, saying, "They have taken away the Lord, and we know not where they have laid him." How often do we sorrow over that which should be a cause of joy! The disciples, excited by the narrative, run to the sepulchre, and find the fact to be as stated by Mary. Peter seems, at first, to have doubted; "for as yet they knew not the Scriptures, that he must rise from the dead." And having satisfied themselves that Jesus was risen, and having now received the doctrine of the resurrection as actually achieved, "the disciples went again to their own homes."

But how different is the conduct of Mary! Moved by stronger affection, she remained behind, chained to the spot where her Savior had lain. The picture, as drawn by the beloved disciple, is touching in the extreme: "She stood without at the sepulchre, weeping; and as she wept, she stooped down and looked into the sepulchre." What a subject for the pencil of an Angelo! The beloved of her soul was crucified, and her heart was broken. There was the spot where had lain his bleeding and torn body; the very spot had a charm for her. Others might go away, and amid other scenes and duties find a balm for their wounded spirits; but to Mary the very grave of her Lord was dear; and thinking that, after all, his body might be there, she stooped down and looked into it. Although deserted by others, and surrounded by dangers calculated to excite her timid heart, yet so completely was she occupied by sorrows for her Savior as to be regardless of all else.

While thus weeping, stooping, desponding, angelic voices address her from the sepulchre, saying, "Woman, why weepest thou?" "Because they have taken away my Lord, and I know not where they have laid him," was the prompt and sorrowing reply. When speaking to the disciples, it was "the Lord;" now it is "my Lord." Love is appropriating. Turning round, she sees in the gray twilight of the morning the outlines of a man, who asks, in rapid succession, "Woman, why weepest thou? whom seekest thou?" Supposing him to be the gardener, she thus passionately addresses him: "Sir, if thou have borne him hence, tell me where thou hast laid him, and I will take him away." Jesus said unto her, "Mary." Startled into ecstasy by the well-known voice, and turning round, she rushes toward him, crying out, "Rabboni," which is to say, "Master." What a subject, again, for the pencil of an Angelo! Forbidding her to touch him, and having announced to her his resurrection, he sent her to his disciples with this message: "Go to my brethren, and say unto them, I ascend unto my Father, and your Father—to my God, and your God." And with her tears all wiped away, and her heart relieved from the weight of its sorrows, and her countenance radiant with commingling joy and hope, she announced to the disciples that she had seen the Lord, and told them the things that he had spoken to her.

We shall now state a few of the lessons taught by this remarkable narrative of this most interesting woman.

1. It teaches us the true effect of saving grace upon the conduct. By saving grace we mean the work of the Spirit renewing the soul after the image of God. This work of the Spirit not only enlightens the understanding, so that spiritual things are seen in a true light, but it also gives the will and the affections an irresistible inclination toward them. It is above nature—it is above moral suasion—it is the effect of the power which created the world.

Connected with this subject are many questions difficult of solution. What is the spirit of man? How does God act upon spirit? In what does the change consist? Christ thus answers these and similar questions: "The wind bloweth where it listeth, and thou hearest the sound thereof, but canst not tell whence it cometh or whither it goeth; so is every one that is born of the Spirit;" that is, you may be ignorant as to the causes and course of the winds, but you see their effects. They move the trees of the forest—they lash the ocean into tempest. The evidences of their power are not unfrequently strown over earth and ocean. And such is the fact as to the Divine influence upon the soul. We may not understand the method of its operation, but the results are read of all men.

How strongly is all this illustrated in the case of Mary! She is described as a poor woman, in the lowest condition of her sex, whose sins were of a crimson dye—as bodily and spiritually under the dominion of Satan. But the possessed of seven devils is made a subject of grace and an heir of glory; and how great the change in her conduct! With the entire devotion of her whole heart she attended upon her Lord. His feet she washed with her mingling tears of pity and joy, and wiped them with the hair of her head, which is the glory of woman. Nor did her affection for him abate when he was accused as a malefactor — when condemned for blasphemy — when crucified between two thieves. She was last at the cross; and having prepared spices for his embalming, she was first at his grave, to perform this last act of affection. The darkness of the night — the danger of the way — the distance from the city—the loneliness of the place—the presence of a rude soldiery excited no fear. No danger could deter her from manifesting her love for her Lord. And such, in kind, is the effect of saving grace upon all hearts. And multitudes of her sex, in every age, have manifested a devotion to the Savior of men only less conspicuous than that of Mary, because less known.

2. It teaches us the honor with which God crowns the exercises of simple faith. Faith is the saving grace. This truth can not be too often asserted in a world where the human heart so universally inclines to the doctrine of merit. "He that believeth in the Lord Jesus Christ shall be saved;" and every instance of the simple exercise of faith should be held forth for universal instruction and imitation.

The case of Mary is a beautiful illustration of it. Her sins were great, but they were freely forgiven; and from the hour of her forgiveness until she passes from our view, her simple faith is conspicuous. She followed her Savior through Judea, sitting at his feet whenever he spoke the words of truth—his instructions falling upon her soul as the rain upon the mown grass. When her Lord was accused as a malefactor, her faith never wavered. She followed him to the hall of Pilate and to the summit of Calvary; and when the last deep groan by which his sufferings were brought to a termination escaped his lips, and his head bowed in death, her faith failed not. When the unbelieving Jews wagged their heads in derision—when the sorrowing disciples went away, not knowing yet but that his death was the end of all they hoped for through him, she stood at a distance gazing upon the scene, mourning, but yet believing. There she stood until Joseph took his body from the cross; nor did she then go away. She followed in the procession to the new-made tomb in the rock, and saw his body wrapped in clean linen and laid away to its burial. While these last offices were performing, she, with the other Mary, sat over against the sepulchre, weeping, but yet believing. Waiting and worshiping through the Sabbath, she hastened to the tomb while it was yet dark, on the morning of the first day of the week, for the purpose of embalming him, undismayed by all the dangers to which she was exposed. Oh Mary, great was thy faith!

And behold the way in which God honors it. As she approached the sepulchre, she found the great stone rolled away from its mouth. Here is one difficulty removed. Looking in vain for her Lord, angels announce to her his resurrection. This glorious truth she is first honored in knowing; she first announces it to his disciples! and she is honored with the first sight of her risen Lord! It is expressly recorded that "he appeared first to Mary Magdalene." What the eye and ear of Jesus had alone seen and heard, he would have recorded to the end of the world; and he would exhibit, in this woman, his peculiar regard for the exercise of simple faith under the most trying circumstances. And to all succeeding generations Mary will stand forth a monument of the blessedness of those who, amid the trials and discouragements of the present mortal state, exercise a simple implicit trust in the Lord.

The Lord is nigh to all those that call upon him. He has graciously promised to be found of all those that seek him aright. Though at all times nigh to those that seek him, he is often hidden from them behind some providential dispensation; but he will soon reveal himself, and teach us, as he did Mary, that they who truly seek him shall not seek him in vain. Clouds can not always obscure the sun. The anger of a kind father does not always burn. Christ is ever more ready to be found of his people than they are to seek him. See him meeting his disciples at the sea when weary with rowing; see him meeting with Daniel when weeping and fasting, and with John when an exile on Patmos. Mary only sought the dead body of her Lord, but she found him alive for evermore, to the joy and rejoicing of her soul! What encouragements to seek the Lord until we find! Weeping may continue for a night, but joy will come in the morning.

3. It teaches us the true way of seeking Christ. When found of Mary, Christ had but just risen; he had not yet ascended. With all the ardor of her soul, she ran to embrace him; but he repels her with what appears, at first sight, an unwonted and unnecessary abruptness, saying to her, "Touch me not." What does this mean? Why thus chill the flow of the warm current of her affections? Mary, perhaps, felt that it was enough for her to find her risen Lord, and was about casting herself at his feet, and clinging to his mere bodily presence. But he means to say to her, "Mary, there is something better than my bodily presence; you must look to a crucified, risen, ascended Savior, and to a sanctifying Spirit; and go tell my brethren that I am risen from the dead — that I am alive for evermore." This we may regard as the meaning of our Lord until we are furnished with a better.

How exactly do Satan, and superstition, and error teach the opposite of all this. They endeavor to attract the mind and the heart from the spiritual to the visible — from the work of Christ to the worship of his pictures and bowing at his name—from heaven to earth—from the truth to the form by which it is expressed. Men are fond of gods which they can see; and hence Satan is ever dressing up something in gaudy trappings, and covering it with gewgaws, and calling it by a religious name, and is ever saying to our sensual race, "These be thy gods, O Israel." But of his devices in these respects we should not be ignorant. To seek Christ aright, we must not look for him in the tomb, nor yet upon the cross, nor yet in the flesh. We must seek him in his word, and rest upon his finished work, and trust to his all-prevalent intercession. Many, like Mary, would cling to his person and presence, but his work for us, and the work of his Spirit in us, alone avail in our behalf as sinners.

In every age, the character of a consummate general and victorious leader of armies has been the glory of man. To return from the field of battle, wearing the wreath of victory, has been considered immortality sufficient; and those who have attained this character have reveled amid the adorations of the multitude. Such was an Alexander, who, after conquering the world, sighed for other worlds to conquer; such was a Cæsar, who, after subduing the enemies of his country, enslaved Rome; such was a Bonaparte,

> "The man of thousand thrones,
> Who strewed our earth with hostile bones,"

and who, by the splendor and rapidity of his achievements, filled the world with his fame. The glory of influencing men by the powers of eloquence, in the senate house, the legislative hall, or in the assemblies of the people, has been intensely sought by man; and a few have attained it. The names of a Demosthenes and a Cicero have become household words. The one awoke Greece to concert against Philip; the other saved his country from the arts of a Catiline; and the forensic fame of a Burke, a Pitt, a Fox, a Henry, a Pinckney, has gone out into all the earth. So the possession of wealth, because of the pomp and circumstances which it sustains, has been the glory of man; and to obtain it, men have dared all dangers, and have searched all climes. But grace is the glory of woman. A true and fervent faith is her crown of glory. These raised Mary from the lowest position of her sex to the very highest to which mortals ever attain. Without these, all the other accomplishments of woman are but "as the flower of the grass."

POPERY IN THE UNITED STATES.*

WHEN we regard all its antecedents, it is no wonder that many of the good people of Britain indulge fears as to the ultimate prevalence of popery in this land. Maryland, one of our oldest states, was settled by papists; Lord Baltimore, its proprietor, was a papist; its first colonists were papists, who fled thither from England in 1633, in order to escape the severity with which they were treated. Papists were thus to Maryland what the Puritans were to New England, and had precisely the same opportunity to impress and to extend their opinions.

Florida, from its settlement by the Spaniards until its cession to the United States in 1820, save a few years of British rule, was entirely under papal influence. There the Spaniards and their priests had every thing at their will as completely as in the neighboring island of Cuba.

The whole country west of the Mississippi, now embracing the states of Louisiana, Arkansas, and Missouri, extending north to Canada, belonged originally to the French, and was settled by them. Indeed, the first Europeans that trod those vast regions were Jesuit missionaries, and never had papal priests a fairer op-

* Written for "The News of the Churches," a monthly paper of great interest, published in Edinburgh.

portunity of laying deep and broad the foundations of their system.

The whole of our northern frontier, from the mouth of the St. Lawrence to Fond du Lac, at the western extremity of Lake Superior, has ever been exposed to the influence of popery from Canada. Indeed, the first settlers of most of the frontier cities and towns along that extended line were papists.

The State of Texas, until its annexation a few years since, was closed against all Protestant influence as strongly as Spain itself; and so was California, until its recent conquest and incorporation with the Union; and it is no wonder, in view of historical statements like these, that many among you may imagine that we are hemmed in on all sides, save on the east, with a popish population, which is pressing inward upon us from the circumference to the centre.

And then, for the last fifty years, there has been a wonderful tide of immigration from the popish countries of Europe pouring itself yearly upon our shores. It is asserted by some popish writers that not less than several millions of Irish immigrants have come hither! Most of these were papists; and Irish papists are to to be found every where in this land; and German papists are now coming hither in numbers, if not surpassing, at least equal to those coming from Ireland, and these very frequently settle in clusters, where they sustain each other in maintaining their national and their religious peculiarities. Now, when we put all these things together, we need not wonder at the fears which many, on your side of the Atlantic, indulge as to the prevalence of popery among us, not at the alarm of many among ourselves on the same subject.

And yet the present facts in the case are as follows: While in Maryland there are only sixty-five papal churches, there are about eight hundred Protestant! While in Florida there are one hundred and fifty-two churches, there are but five of them papal! Of the two hundred and seventy-eight churches of Louisiana, but fifty-five belong to the Pope! Already there are one hundred and sixty-four churches in Texas, of which but thirteen are papist! and at the present hour, the Protestant is, beyond all odds, the predominant influence in California, where, until very recently, Romanism reigned supreme and alone! Indeed, the census just published by Congress reveals the fact that the papists have in the entire country, from the Atlantic to the Pacific, but eleven hundred and twelve churches, accommodating 621,000 hearers, which is not one eleventh of the number of Methodist churches, scarcely one eighth of the Baptist, and not one fourth of the Presbyterian. I hope these statistics, drawn with some care from the last census lying before me, may be remembered and pondered on the other side of the water.

And the moral influence of our papal population is far below what might be expected from its numerical strength. Its political power lies in the fact that the dupes of the system vote at the bidding of the priest; and the priest would lead his followers to the polls to vote for Beelzebub as president, governor, or mayor, if he would only subserve his purposes. On this account the different political parties court the priest in public, in order to secure the votes of his followers, while they detest him in private. But, as it is a poor rule that does not work both ways, this power is rapidly passing away, for our politicians are beginning to see that to court the papist is to array against them the Protestant; and there is nothing to be gained by this operation, as the Protestant is to the papist as twelve to one. While their political power is thus going, their moral power is nothing. The people are generally poor and ignorant, and greatly immoral. They are, as a rule, our only beggars. They are the keepers of our low grog-shops and tippling-houses; they form the main staple of our alms-houses, and of our jails and prisons. A few days since, an examination was made in the House of Correction in South Boston, and out of forty boys there confined for crime, thirty-eight were the children of popish parents. And from the fact that priests are usually the attendants of those executed for murder, I infer that most of our high criminals have been brought up amid the debasing and demoralizing influences of popery. It is with us as it is every where else in the world, the more intense the popery, the more intense the ignorance and wickedness of the people.

Nor do popish priests or periodicals give any moral power to the system. They have but few men of any talent, and these have been so thoroughly beaten in the fields of oral and written discussion as to greatly diminish their influence even with their own people. Bishop Hughes, of New York, has been the most forward of all the priests, and, because of his political influence with the Irish, was not a little dreaded; but his prestige is all gone, and his character as a controvertist is in the dust. Their papers, too, are of a low order, conducted mainly to excite the passions of the people, and to inflame their prejudices; so that from the ministry and the press, which are towers of strength to the evangelical Christians of this land, popery gains nothing but weakness.

And there are special causes existing at this moment which make very much against the entire system. I will briefly allude to a few of them.

The visit of Gavazzi had a wonderful effect in drawing attention to the opposition of the system to the progress of human liberty. Multitudes thronged every where to hear him, and his orations had a powerful effect in arousing the public mind to the enormities and the wickedness of the priests; and the fierce riots with which he was greeted in Montreal by the Irish papists greatly increased his power.

The persecutions abroad have been considered and pondered here. They are denounced by the press all over the Union, save the few in the pay of the priests; and the vindication by these of the conduct of the Tuscan government, in the case of the Madiai and Miss Cunninghame, has powerfully reacted against them. There is nothing on which we are so intensely sensitive as on persecution for opinion's sake; and it is known by us all, that in the vocabulary of the papist, "freedom of opinion on matters of religious concernment" is synonymous with licentiousness, and is a damnable delusion.

There is a little island, Cuba, lying south of Florida,

and within a few days' sail of New York, which is constantly giving us illustrations of the spirit of popery. Our people go there in the winter for health, and return in the spring to tell us of the immoralities of the priests, and the intense superstition and bigotry of the people, and of the enormous impositions of the Church; and when we need in any way an illustration of the spirit of popery, we need only point to Cuba, worse governed at this hour than probably any spot in Europe or America. Scenes are there of weekly occurrence, under the dictation of the Church, which are a disgrace to the civilized world.

The debates in some of our Legislatures, and the discussion in many of our papers as to "the property question," has reacted powerfully on the priests. Here our individual churches are held by trustees, who are elected annually, and who are known in law as a body corporate. The priests have sought to have an act passed making the bishop of the diocese the sole trustee of all Church property. They fear to trust their people; and as the bishops are appointed by the Pope, such a law would place an immense amount of property to be used, through his pliant tools, at will, by the Holy Father. This effort has arrayed many papists against the priests, who have been signally defeated in their object, and has done much to expose their vaulting ambition. Every such effort, in its failure, has a destructive rebound.

And last, though not least, in these adverse causes, may be named the visit of Bedini, the Pope's Nuncio to Brazil, taking the United States on his way! He came here a wolf in the clothing of a sheep, and when the clothing which covered him was taken off, he was treated as a wolf. When it was known who he was, the Italians and Germans rose against him as the butcher of Bologna, and he had to flee the country to save his life. His great dread was from his own countrymen, who saw upon his hand and on his robes the blood of their own compatriots; so that the very men from whom we might expect an importation of Austrian and Italian popery are the very men who scared the nuncio out of his senses, and caused him to flee as an assassin from a land where he expected to be treated as a prince. The rebound upon popery is tremendous, and the priests are at their wits' ends to know what to do. The sun upon their dial has gone fifty years backward.

So that you need not fear in Britain as to the prevalence of popery in the United States. Let the Irish and the Continental papists come; we have room for them all. We would have no objection to the coming of the Pope himself. Unless he can outpreach us, we have no dread of him; and when he does that in truth, he ought to succeed.

To a few of the causes which have led to these results I now ask your attention.

1. Emigration itself tends to expand, enlarge, and liberalize the mind. The peasants of Europe are poor, attached to ancient habits, and as far forth as they are papists, bigoted, superstitious, and the dupes of the priest. Such are benefited by a journey from the interior of Ireland to Belfast or Dublin; and when they

return home they have many new subjects of thought. But when they cross the Atlantic, and become citizens of the Western World, there is soon a great revolution apparent. They have seen the wide sea; they are mixing up with a new people. New objects arrest attention; new pursuits occupy their minds and their hands. They are no longer serfs or tenants; for the most menial employment they receive full wages. They soon exchange their brogues for shoes, their caps for bonnets, their breeches for pantaloons, their frieze for broadcloth. And there is a similar internal revolution. They commence thinking for themselves. The bands of superstition relax, and soon fall from around them. The dread of the priest has passed away, and in proportion of the severity of the bondage of the fatherland is the rapidity with which they break away from it. As the feelings and habits of Turk or Jew would be greatly modified by a residence in Scotland, so are those of papists by a residence in America. And here is an influence which no priestly vigilance can arrest. I found a young and vigorous papist reading some tracts which I once scattered over a vessel at sea. "Why is it," said I, "that you read Protestant tracts?" "I have been three years in America, and I have learned to think for myself," was the reply. The whole history of emigration proves that it tends to the modification of opinions, habits, and customs. Nor is it possible for the papist to be here what he was in Ireland, France, or Austria.

2. And every man in this land reads and thinks for himself, when he can read or think at all. The popu-

lar institutions of the country render it necessary to discuss all subjects before the people, and hence the all-pervading extent of the political press. Every body reads the papers, and the papers discuss every thing; and books and periodicals are rained down all over the land; and such is the pressure in that direction, that a man is almost as much compelled to read here as he is to go forward when drawn or driven by a locomotive. And the priest can not select the matter to be read by his people. The mass-book is soon laid aside for the newspaper, and "The Lives of the Saints," that compound of lying wonders, for miscellaneous reading; and but few here take any thing on credit. The father and son are very often on the opposite sides of the political and religious creed. The American feeling is to sift evidence for ourselves, and to receive nothing as an article of faith simply because our fathers received it. The priest that would attempt to fasten his dogmas upon a youth born here, simply because they were believed by his parents, would soon find himself in the vocative. He would soon be told that his argument, if valid, would keep the Turk a Turk, the Jew a Jew, the heathen a heathen forever. This American feeling makes our country a very hard one for popish missionaries. The traditionary argument, strong in Ireland and Italy, is here as flax before the fire, as dry stubble before the raging conflagration.

3. Because of the entire separation between the Church and the state, we have no legal enactment of any kind for the support of religion. The laws protect

the Sabbath, and they protect every man—the Hindu equally with the papist and Protestant in his religious worship. No man is compelled to support any faith or worship in any way or form. Hence we have no dissenters—no clashing of parties for patronage—no jealousies of sects because of governmental favors. Hence the trade of the priest in Ireland is destroyed here; and he can no more get up a crusade against the Protestants on legal grievances than he can get up a procession of the host in New York, like those of Rome or Naples. This gives a great advantage; for as they stand on equal ground with us before the law, there is no excited passion to blind them to the force of our arguments. We are thus thrown upon the Bible and our principles, and those only who have Scripture and reason on their side can have any hope of success. Here we have a vast advantage.

Although an excitable, we are, after all, a very common-sense people. Things that seem very proper among you would expose a man here to intense ridicule. An advocate who would go into one of our courts with a wig on his head, as among you, would never get over it. It is as much as many of our Apostolical Successionists and our Baptismal Regenerators can do to get cleverly along. When impervious to reason, they are intensely ridiculed; but when the nonsense assumes the shape of popery, and in that form puts forward its dogmas and pretensions, it revolts our common sense. Such is the wakefulness of our people to all subjects, that even servants in the kitchen, mechanics in the shop, workmen on our railways and canals, discuss and decide upon high topics which engaged the minds of Aquinas and Bellarmine; and, when Scripture and reason fail, the cause is lost, and the doctrine is surrendered. Hence the multitudes that have left the papal Church, and the multitudes yet nominally attached to it, who believe in Purgatory, and priestly remissions, and praying to saints, and in the mummery of the mass, just as much as you Scotch Presbyterians believe in the saintship of Claverhouse or in the authenticity of the Apocrypha.

4. Every nation has its own peculiar tastes. This is so as to the fine arts, as to architecture, dress, and the mechanic arts; and while true religion is every where the same, because consisting in a right state of the heart toward God, yet there are natural tastes as to its external development. There may be said to be in religion an Italian, German, French, English, and Scotch taste. And why not an American? The showy robes of English prelacy, which are venerated south of the Tweed, are regarded as the rags of "the old lady on the seven hills" north of it; and the plain, simple dress of the north is disdained in the south. The American feeling tends strongly to the simple in religion, so that even the gown and bands are all but universally laid aside among all Protestants, save Episcopalians; and their dress and forms are among the great obstructions to their growth as a people. If for no other reasons than these, they never can extend as do other branches of the Church in this land. Hence the taste of the country is most decidedly anti-papal. Popery might do for the Dark Ages—it may do for a

semi-enlightened people — it may do as a system of police in the old nations of Europe—it may do to maintain the authority of the priest over an ignorant people — it may do for Italy, or for Austria, or for infidel France, or for groaning Ireland, but it is not adapted to America; the national taste is averse to it, and just in proportion as emigrants here become Americans do they become anti-papists. The religion of Italy can never intrench itself in the American heart; its history, its claims, its pretensions, its lying wonders, are no greater obstacles to its growth than are the intelligence, the common sense, and the taste of our people.

5. The Bible and the common school are mighty causes for good among us. It is doubtful if there is a people on the globe, as numerous as we are, among whom the Bible is more generally circulated. There is a crying destitution, I admit, but it is mostly among emigrants, and on the selvages of the country, where Christian enterprise has followed too tardily in the wake of our extending population; and as we are not afraid of the Douay Bible, we ask the papist why he should be afraid of ours? We tell him that we will take his Bible, if it has an almanac at the end of it; if half of it is omitted; if it is badly translated; and we ask him why he will not take ours, even if he believes it defective in some points? We moreover tell him that we wish him to believe no doctrine which is not plainly taught in his version and ours. And the Bible is read by papists in thousands; nor can the anathemas of the priests do any thing, save to stimulate them onward to its perusal. We tell them that the Bible is

a letter from their heavenly Father directed to them, and for the priest to claim the right to read it for them, and to tell them what is in it, is as preposterous as to claim to read and to interpret for them the letters sent to them by earthly parents. And this is to them both an illustration and an argument, the force of which they strongly feel. When they seriously read the Bible, it is all over with the Pope and the priest.

And then, in most of our states there is a system of public schools, by which all the children are brought together for instruction. In these schools the children of the governor and of his coachman, of the papist and of the Protestant, meet. They sit on the same bench, read the same books, and receive the same instruction. Their minds come into conflict; and they grow up together to think and to act for themselves. If the Bible is not read, nor a word said upon religious topics in these schools, their whole drift and tendency is anti-papal. This the priests plainly see; and hence their bitter and leagued opposition to our public schools. Knowledge is to these youths what a knife is in the hands of a man bound with ropes—it enables them to cut the ties of prejudice and superstition by which they are fettered; and the priests publicly declare that it is better for papal parents to permit their children to grow up in abject ignorance, than to send them to these schools, where their salvation is so much jeopardized! But parents will send their children to school. They see that there is no other hope for their rising above the condition of menials, and they will breast the wrath of the priest, which, even here, is sometimes quite fierce, rather than fasten the yoke of servitude on their children by bringing them up in ignorance. So that between the Bible and our common schools, the priests have a hard time of it. The one is the upper, and the other is the nether stone of a mill which we keep in vigorous operation. We put the children in at the hopper, and they come out at the spout Americans and Protestants. Hence the children of papal parents, educated here, to a remarkable extent pass over from the superstitious faith of their fathers.

Indeed, the very atmosphere of our country is Protestant. You see it and feel it every where. It infuses a new kind of life into the papists coming here. Even the priests skulk from the light which blazes around them, and show by their downcast looks that they are doing the deeds of darkness. Hence they must be all imported. Priests of native birth are about as scarce as bats in winter; and even the ordinary servants, when asked as to their religion, often hesitate, and when papists, seemed ashamed to own it.

These are some of the causes why popery is in its present low and feeble condition in the United States, in view of its history, its opportunities, and its antecedents; and these causes are yearly increasing in force and number. And never did it stand in such a pitiable plight before the country as it does at this hour.

I promise you that if you take care of papists in Britain, we will take care of them in America.

A DREAM.

It was the week of the anniversaries in New York, and when they were mostly celebrated in Metropolitan Hall. With others, I crowded my way to that gorgeously-decorated building, since laid in ashes, and heard several addresses of a mixed and varied character, as they have been, and must be. Some of them were wise, and some otherwise; some were very flat—some very inflated; some advocate the particular charity, and some themselves in particular. When the powers of sitting and hearing were both exhausted, I left the Hall, and wandered about, I cared not whither, until, rousing to some observation, I found myself in Brooklyn. There a raree show attracted my attention, the actors in which were young men and women, exquisitely dressed, wonderfully polite and fascinating, and passionately enamored of one another. I stood and gazed upon their frivolous and amorous antics for some time, when I was beckoned behind the curtain, and entered. I soon found that I was among females of the most fascinating manners, but of loose conversation and morals, and in a room elegantly furnished. I was left alone with some maidens, whose lips dropped as a honeycomb, and whose tempting words were smoother than oil. A parley commenced; their temptations were resisted, and, resenting the deception practiced on me, I fled the room.

I made my exit through a room filled with vulgar men, who were drinking, smoking, swearing, and indulging in boisterous mirth. I wrapped my cloak around me so as to conceal my person, unwilling, pure and innocent as I was, to be recognized as having been even decoyed into such a place. But as I passed out, I heard a low whisper pass round the room, and obviously uttered with glee, "There goes a minister! there goes a minister!" A feeling of shame and humiliation came over me, and I drew my cloak more tightly around my neck and face as I issued from the den of wickedness—from the house built upon the highway to hell.

A few men, who seemed to act as spies upon the house, and determined to know the names of its visitors, met me at the door. They sought a view of my face in a way I deemed inquisitive and impertinent, and asked me my name. I returned a sharp reply, and so as to rebuke their impertinence. "You are a minister," they said, "and we will find out who you are, at any rate or cost." I was shocked alike by their recognition of my calling and their stern resolution. I saw in a moment they were men not to be turned aside from their purpose. I passed through narrow streets—I entered public houses by one door and went out by another, but those iron men followed me; and when rejoicing that I had at length escaped from them, I would meet them at the next corner, as determined as ever to find me out. "We will find you out," were the words with which they greeted me at every meeting. I went up the river—I entered a narrow lane—I concealed myself amid a thick grove of trees at its end, and when hoping they had lost my trail, they stood before me, saying, "We will find you out." I eventually gained a narrow neck of land, almost surrounded by water, and covered with all kinds of rubbish, amid which there were many low trees. Not an individual was there, and I could readily conceal myself from any one seeking me from the water or from the land. Here I hid myself, now among old logs, now amid low trees, until I hoped my pursuers had given over all search of me; but the moment I issued from it, they were the first to meet me, and sternly to say to me, "We will find you out." I entered a ferry-boat to cross the river; they were behind me; they told every body they saw me coming out of a house of very suspicious character, and asked all on board if they knew me. All eyes were scrutinizing me, and yet none recognized me.

When landed in New York, my pursuers entered into a conversation with friends they met on the wharf, saying they were going to have a great Moral Reform meeting that evening at Metropolitan Hall, and that they were going over to secure the services, if possible, of the Rev. Dr. ———, of ———. "Why," said the persons, "Dr. ——— was on board the boat with you; why did you not ask him there?"

"Where is he?" they quickly asked.

"There he is, with the cloak round his neck," was the reply.

"And is that Dr. ——— ?" said they, with astonishment; "why, we saw him coming out of a suspicious house in Brooklyn but a short time ago, and we suspected he was a minister, and we told him we would find him out. And is that Dr. ——— ?" They seemed amazed, and confounded, and overwhelmed; for, although very prying persons, they seemed to be good men.

I was now discovered; and, although conscious of innocence, I felt there was an appearance of evil which I could not satisfactorily explain, and I was, in my turn, overwhelmed with confusion. My conduct was almost sufficient to prove my guilt; instead of denouncing the house, and the deception practiced on me, and frankly telling my name to those men at once, I acted as if a guilty man. Rousing to a sense of my position, and recognizing, though late, that honesty was the best policy, I walked up to the men, threw aside my cloak, declared my name, and just as, with earnest soul, I commenced a true narrative of all the circumstances, I awoke, and, to my unutterable joy, found that it was all a dream.

The whole thing created a nervous excitement, which prevented any further sleep that night. Although a dream, it had its lessons of instruction, which I pondered and noted, and which, on the next day, I committed to writing for my own benefit. They are now published for the benefit of others.

1. It teaches us to beware of all allurements which would decoy us into the ways of sin. The fly plays unsuspiciously around the candle; first its wings are

scorched, and then it falls into the burning flame. The spider weaves its beautiful web, and when insects fall into its meshes, the venomous weaver gloats upon their struggles, seizes them in its deadly fangs, and carries them away to its dark cell. And thus often are men decoyed from the ways of virtue, and scarcely know where they are until those deeds are committed which bite like a serpent, and sting like an adder.

2. It teaches us how much we need grace in the hour of temptation. Wicked persons are cowards when resisted; but, once yield to their solicitations, and they are bold as a lion. It is difficult to drag a boat from the land to the water; but when out on the water, the hand of a child may drive it along and turn it in any direction. Man, in his virtue, is strong; but when he lets down its bars, the lock of his strength is gone, and he is in the lap of Delilah, and exposed to the Philistines.

3. It teaches us promptly and honestly to meet all accusers face to face. When accused of an evil done, frankly confess it, repent of it, and forsake the way which leads to its repetition; when wrongly accused, assert your innocence, even when circumstances may be such as to excite suspicion. Suspicious circumstances may be explained, but a cowardly evasion of explanation may be tantamount to proof. Joseph asserted his innocence even when the wife of Potiphar produced his garment in testimony against him.

4. It teaches us to avoid the appearance of evil. Although entirely innocent, appearances may be strongly against us, and, in the absence of positive testimony,

the world relies on the evidence of appearances; especially is this so when the character of Christians is involved. Hence the point and the importance of the command, "Abstain from all appearance of evil."

And that low whisper which passed round the room, and was uttered with so much apparent joy, "There goes a minister! there goes a minister!" proves and illustrates the way and manner in which the sins of the good cheer and strengthen the wicked in their iniquity. Sin is essentially agrarian; it would reduce all to its own base level; and the pillars of the temple of religion and virtue are giving way when the ministers of God fall into sin. No doubt the example of David, in multitudes of instances, is quoted in mitigation of the sin of adultery down to the present day.

So that even from dreams many instructive lessons may be drawn.

K

THE PRAYER OF FAITH.

In my early ministry, "the Prayer of Faith" was a topic of frequent and earnest discussion. Fanatical and greatly erroneous views had widely obtained in reference to it, and mainly through the agency of a wandering class of evangelists, who for a time were greatly popular, but who, happily, have now passed away like the summer brook. If a congregation was not revived, it was because the minister and people had no faith; if prayers were not immediately answered, it was because they were not offered in faith; if the children of pious parents were not converted, it was because they were not prayed for in faith; and if all things for which we are commanded to pray were not just as God would have them, the fault was laid, by those fanatical evangelists, at the door of the Church, and to its lack of faith. And many a story did they narrate as to the efficacy of their prayers, in proof and illustration of their positions; and by these evangelists and their followers, those ministers who enjoyed no revivals, and those Christian parents whose children were unconverted, were denounced as faithless, and all who opposed their measures and their views were regarded as formalists, and as blind leaders of the blind.

And all this, among the sincere and pious, was owing, perhaps, as much to a misinterpretation of Scripture as to any other cause. We are obviously taught that there were two kinds of faith in the early Church —extraordinary, or the faith of miracles; and common, which was exercised by all who believed the Gospel. The faith of miracles was exercised by many who were never truly converted, as by Judas; but common faith, in its very nature, is a gracious exercise. These often met in the same person, but they are clearly different from one another. The faith of miracles was peculiar to those who wrought them, and included not only belief in the being and attributes of God, but also that a particular miracle would be wrought. And so Christ teaches, "Whatsoever things ye desire, when you pray, believe that ye receive them, and ye shall have them." And without here entering into the question as to how this faith was excited in the soul, we only assert that in the exercise of it every thing that was asked was granted. Hence the promise, "The prayer of faith shall save the sick," which is simply a promise that miraculous effects should follow a prayer preferred in the exercise of miraculous faith.

Besides this, there is a faith common to all Christians, which rests simply on the word and promises of God. It is the fruit and the effect of Divine teaching, and is wrought in the soul by the Holy Ghost. This faith rests on the being, the power, the promises, the wisdom, the benevolence of God. In its exercise we go to God as children to a kind and living father, knowing that he will give to us what we need and will be for our good, and that he will withhold only what we do not need and what would injure. The prayer of faith, as now offered, consists in going to God, believing that he is, and that he is the rewarder of those who diligently seek him, and in the full persuasion that no good thing will he withhold from them that walk uprightly. It consists in casting all our care upon him, knowing that he careth for us.

Such is truly the prayer of faith; and because failing to distinguish between the faith of miracles and ordinary faith, as exercised by all believers in prayer, many have become vain and clamorous fanatics, acting as if God were bound to grant them whatever they asked with a zeal inflamed to scalding heat. The true model of the prayer of faith we have in the prayer of our Savior in the garden of agony, with the tragedy and sufferings of Calvary in full view, "Abba, Father, all things are possible unto thee; take away this cup from me; nevertheless, not what I will, but what thou wilt." Here was the prayer of faith offered by the Son of Man himself for the instruction and the imitation of all believers.

In one of the northern counties of the State of Pennsylvania there lived an aged man, honored and beloved by all that knew him for his piety, intelligence, integrity, and kind philanthropy. His life was a living evidence to the truth and power of religion, which the most bitter infidel could not gainsay. He had but one child, and that child was a son, at the head of a large family of his own, and living at the distance of some miles from the house of his father. He was a frank, honest, generous man, but was living without hope and without God. He was laid upon a bed of sickness, and his disease soon put forth fatal symptoms. The aged father was summoned to the bed of his son; and as he felt his jumping pulse, and laid his hand upon his burning brow, and was informed that all hopes of his recovery were surrendered, he was intensely moved. He soon retired alone to a room, where, in agony of spirit, he wrestled with God for the life of his only son. Dejected and mourning, he returned to the bed of sickness, and spoke to his son, as he could, about Jesus, and repentance, and faith, and salvation. But, to his surprise and deep regret, that dying son heard all he had to say without the least emotion. The fever somewhat abated, and hopes were indulged, but it was only to return with greater violence. The father again repaired to that room, and again he wrestled with God, and again, dejected and mourning, he returned to speak to his son about Jesus and the resurrection. But his tears, instructions, exhortations, made no impression. Again the broken-hearted father repaired to that room of audience with Deity, where he remained a long while; and when he again appeared at the dying bed, it was with a spirit and manner entirely changed. His heart seemed joyful, though sad; he conversed cheerfully with all. A calm succeeded to the intense excitement which convulsed his whole soul, as does the tempest the ocean. Soon the dying man became deeply anxious about his salvation; his father and his pastor pointed him to the cross; they explained to him the nature of faith, and unfolded the promise and the command, "Believe on the Lord Jesus Christ, and thou shalt be saved." He believed; his life was protracted for a few days, through which he gave as strong evidence as the circumstances would admit that he was renewed by the power of the Holy Ghost; and he died in the arms of his aged father, saying, with his last breath, "I know, when this earthly house of my tabernacle is dissolved, I will have a building of God, a house not made with hands, eternal in the heavens."

The composure of the aged father was so great after that protracted visit to the room of prayer, and his whole demeanor was so changed, as to excite attention. A calm serenity marked his conduct during the death-struggle and the funeral solemnities; and when turning away from the grave, he said, with tears, but yet with joy, "The Lord gave, and the Lord hath taken away; blessed be the name of the Lord." And on being asked to give an account of his exercises during these last days of his dying son, he gave the following narrative:

"When I first heard of the sickness of my son, I could not even suppose that he was going to die; but when I first stood by his bedside, my heart sunk within me. I saw that no power but that of God could hold him back from the grave; and I went to my room to pray for him, and I sought for his life with a heart that would admit of no denial. But God seemed hid from me, and I was troubled. I went again with very much the same feeling, and with the same request. I could not bear to think of the death of my son, and especially in his unprepared state; and my heart seemed dried, yes, withered within me, and I returned unsatisfied. But I did not feel aright; I was unwilling that God should have his own way. I examined my feelings, and I thought of God. So I went to my room again, and I soon found that I could talk with God as a man converses with a friend. I told him that for that son I prayed before he was born, and daily since; that I devoted him in his infancy to his Creator; that I sought to bring him up in the ways of religion; and while I confessed my deficiencies, I plead his promises. I sought his life, if consistent with the will of God; but if that could not be granted, I then asked the Lord to hold him back from the grave until he was prepared to make an exchange of worlds. Then, after pouring out my full soul, I left my dear son in the hands of my God, perfectly satisfied that he would do what was right and wise with him and with me, and desirous that the will of God should be accomplished, whether by his life or by his death. My murmuring heart was then at rest. I felt that God would answer my many prayers on his behalf. When I heard his crying for mercy — his rejoicing in the Lord, it was what I expected; and then I was satisfied that he should die; and now I know that while he can not return to me, I must soon go up to him, and I am only waiting for my Master to say, 'Come up hither.' But that wrestling with God, when I thought I could lay hold on his strength, will be ever a memorable point in my history."

That was the prayer of faith; and we offer the

prayer of faith when we pray, believing in the being and attributes of God—in the truth of his promises—that he will withhold nothing which he deems best for them which they ask agreeably to his will, and which they implore through Jesus Christ, through whom all gracious blessings are bestowed. Such is the prayer of faith; and this is the prayer which moves the hand which moves the world.

DEATH-BED REPENTANCES.

As we sin daily, repentance should be the work of every day; and as we are by nature the children of wrath, repentance and faith are the only means of escaping the wrath of God denounced against sin. These are to sinners what planks are to sailors after shipwreck, upon which they may escape to the shore, or in the neglect of which they must perish amid the roaring billows.

There is no duty more frequently presented in the Scriptures, and none to which we are more frequently urged by conscience, than repentance; and yet there is none which we are more frequently inclined to postpone. When sin once takes up its lodgings in the heart, it is difficult to dispossess it, and hence the disposition to put off repentance to another day. But it should be remembered that he that has promised life on repentance has not promised life until we repent; and that if we repent not in his time, he may not accept of it when it suits our interests to render it. While true repentance is never too late, late repentances are seldom sincere.

Hence the awful delusion of putting off repentance to a sick-bed and to the last hours of life. To give up the world when we can no longer use it — to mourn over passions that we can no longer indulge — to express sorrow for sins when just going to the tribunal where we must meet them all, would seem, on the face of the statement, to be fatal to our sincerity; and then to build up hopes upon such repentances, in the great majority of cases, is like building a house upon vapors which vanish before the sunlight, or upon the ice which dissolves before the first breath of summer. And however true and sincere, because there is no time to test them, death-bed repentances, in the nature of the case, must be ever unsatisfactory to surviving friends; and the return of those to sin on their restoration to health, who, when all hope of life was given up, seemed truly penitent and prepared to meet their God, goes very far to cast a very deep shade over all such repentings, and should induce all ministers to protest against them, and should lead all men to conclude that the Ethiopian is not thus usually washed white—that the spots of the leopard are not thus easily removed. In my whole ministerial experience of twenty-five years, I remember but one case of severe sickness, which was supposed to be unto death, that resulted in true repentance, and in a new life on recovery.

There was a gay, dashing young man under my early ministry, the son of pious parents, who had passed into the skies, leaving him, in early life, to be cared for by others, who did not neglect him. He was taken sick, and of a lingering disease, which seemed steadily pursuing its fatal purpose. I soon became a visitor, and then a daily attendant upon him. His sins came up in order before him, and he was intensely anxious about his salvation. Nothing, for many days, could soothe his disturbed feelings. I sat by his side, resolved, as far as possible, to remove every doubt and every objection from the Bible which I held open in my hand. He urged his great sinfulness. I pointed to Manasseh, David, Paul, who found mercy; and told him of John Bunyan, and of many cases which passed under my own observation. He feared that Christ would not receive him. I told him of the errand of Christ to seek and to save the lost; I taught him as to the way in which the salvation of sinners added to the declarative glory of the Savior. When all objections were removed, and when his fears were thus quelled, I placed the plan of salvation in its simplicity and efficacy before him, and urged his acceptance of it; and before I closed my Bible, he said, "Well, I never saw things before in this light; I think I can thus receive and rest upon Christ for salvation." I prayed with him, and retired.

At my next visit he was rejoicing in Christ, and in the most familiar manner narrating his new feelings to his friends. The disease steadily progressed until I expected daily to hear of his death, but there seemed not a waver in his feeling of confidence in Christ. His spiritual joy increased with his feebleness, until he longed to depart and to be with Christ. His feelings, at times, rose up into the region of rapture. He selected his funeral text and hymn, and talked freely and peaceably about his departure; and although my confidence in such conversions was always weak, yet I felt that this was a genuine case, and so spoke of it to many.

To the amazement of all, a change, as if by miracle, took place in his disease, and he commenced slowly to recover. My visits became less frequent, and with returning health there came a dryness of conversation on religious subjects. At each visit I could mark a declension, until finally there was a reluctance to hear any thing personal on the subject. When I saw him for the first time, weak and wan, in the street, and tottering on the top of a stick, I approached to congratulate him on his getting out again; but, observing me, he turned into an alley. Often did he send for me when sick, but now, when recovering, he avoided me. He soon regained his usual strength, and returned to his ordinary pursuits, and, as if for the purpose of erasing all impressions of his sick-bed repentings, he went to every excess of riot. Before his sickness he was wild, now he was wicked; before, he was a decent rowdy, now he was a drunken rake; before, he was full of noisy nonsense, now you could hear his boisterous profanity all over the street. He openly scoffed at God, at the Bible, at religion in all its forms; and whenever he saw me approaching him in the street, he always crossed to the opposite side, ashamed to meet one who had so often bowed with him in prayer while apparently on the crumbling verge of eternity, and to whom he so often expressed spiritual hopes and joys, which, in the belief of their sincerity, caused me to thank God and take courage.

No case of repentance on the borders of the grave ever inspired me with greater confidence, and in no case of backsliding were my hopes so utterly dashed.

Many years have passed away since I saw this young man. Whether he has gone—whether living or dead, I know not; but when I last saw him, he was as far from the kingdom of heaven as any person I ever knew. And yet, had he died of that fearful sickness, I would have held him up as an instance of true conversion on a dying-bed. "Man looketh on the outward appearance, but the Lord looketh on the heart."

From very many similar instances I select another. Mr. B—— was an active, skillful mechanic, of bright mind, ready wit, and free, social habits. But he was profane, given to drink, skeptical, and neglectful of all religious ordinances. I often sought to make some serious impression in some way upon him, but I was only beating the air. He fell into a slow consumption; and while he could go about, my visits to him in sickness were like those in health, apparently in vain. When his lungs were almost gone, and on a very warm day in summer, when the air was motionless and filled with vapor, and when even those in perfect health felt oppressed, he sent for me. I found him gasping for breath, and apparently dying. He, in broken accents, confessed his great sins, and implored forgiveness of God. I told him of Christ, and of the freeness of his salvation to all who truly repented and believed. "Oh," said he, "I repent and believe with all my heart." I told him that all God required was the heart, and that when we believed with the heart the justifying righteousness of Christ was ours. "I believe with all my heart," was his energetic reply. I prayed with him, and retired, deeply pondering the event.

I called next day and found him considerably relieved, but yet breathing with difficulty. I made kind inquiries as to his symptoms. "Oh," said he, "there is nothing the matter with me but these d—d lungs," at the same time striking his breast with great violence; "they are getting better, and I hope to be soon out again." I was shocked at his profanity. I sought to recall the feelings and confessions of the previous day, but, inspired by his temporary relief with the hope of recovery, it was all in vain. The heart, which, in the presence of death, had melted as wax before the fire, had resumed its accustomed icy hardness and coldness. Fear had inspired his feelings; and when fear subsided, his feelings passed away like foam upon the troubled waters.

But soon death came again, and with a determination not to be driven from his prey. I was again summoned in a great hurry to his dying bed. He was in the last struggle. The big, cold sweat came gushing from all his pores. He strove to speak, but in vain. He looked on me imploringly, and with a keen earnestness which made impressions now as fresh as when made, though years have passed away. I held up Christ to him, dwelling upon the text, "Look unto me, all ye ends of the earth, and be ye saved." I told him that, though he could not speak nor turn, yet he could look—that it was only to "look and live." He understood all—he assented to all. And he died, leaving on my heart the deep impression that all his religious feelings were induced by the fear of death, and that if he had recovered, his confessions and prayers would have been subjects of mirth while occupying a seat among the scorners, and among the fools that hate knowledge. Instances like these have taught me,

1. To place no strong confidence in death-bed repentances. Even when they are such as to inspire some hope, I say but little about them. I would not rudely tear away the comfort they give to surviving friends, but I carefully refrain from making them the basis of hope to any. Before God they may be genuine, but before man they must ever be doubtful, as we must judge of repentance by its fruits.

2. They have taught me to warn all men against postponing repentance to a dying bed. Repentance is the work of our life, and of every day of it. And to put it aside until we can sin no more among our fellow-men, until the last sands in the glass of life are running, is unutterably preposterous. When men make their will in health, why will they put off repentance to sickness and a dying bed? Are the favors of God —our eternal residence, matters of such inferior importance as to be crowded into the last hours of life, and when utterly unable to attend to earthly things?

True, the thief on the cross repented, and was pardoned in the last hour of his life, but we do not know that he ever had, previously, a call to repentance. Had he been frequently called, and had he frequently refused to attend, we have no reason to conclude that he would have been called again. The most hopeless of men are those who have most frequently quenched the Spirit, and who have most frequently turned a deaf ear to the calls of mercy. Iron is converted into steel by being frequently hardened and suddenly cooled; and thus the heart of steel is made. The only sure way to secure a truly peaceful and happy death is to live the life of the righteous. The thief on the cross is the only instance of true repentance, at the close of life, in the Bible, and that is placed on record to forbid presumption and despair. If but one such case is on record, who should presume? If one is on record, who need despair?

DIFFERENT OPERATIONS—THE SAME SPIRIT.

There are many ministers who are very fond of relating religious experiences in their preaching; there are meetings among some evangelical Christians for the special purpose of narrating experiences; and in the religious literature of the Church, there are many truthful and deeply-interesting narratives of the conversion of men who subsequently became greatly distinguished in life, and which are held up as almost the only truthful models; and there is a great tendency to test our own experience by these, rather than by the law and the testimony; and the more peculiar any experience may be, the more many regard it as genuine, and the more anxious are they that their own should be a counterpart of it. That wonderful book, the Pilgrim's Progress, portrays in many of its thrilling scenes the experience of Bunyan himself, because of his previous life and peculiar temperament, one of the most tempted of the children of God; and I have known many humble and devoted disciples, because their experience was different from that of Christian, living in the constant fear that they had neither lot nor part among the children of light. Because of the influence of natural temperament on our experience, and of our disposition to regard that as the most genuine which is the most marked by extremes, I have sometimes doubted whether these narratives were productive of most good or evil. Because some could tell the day, the place, the circumstances of their conversion, I have known others, giving far more evidence of a new nature, mourning because they could not. Because men of nervous and feeble frames were at times in the deepest gloom, I have heard good people, who were the salt of the earth, often questioning their own state because they had no feelings corresponding to those of the sainted Brainerd and Payson. And just as travelers love to visit the dashing river, whose rapids delight, and whose cataracts astonish and overwhelm, rather than the deep, quiet one which pursues its noiseless way to the ocean, so good people prefer to read and ponder the experience to which a peculiar mind and temper give exciting variety, rather than that of those whose lives are only marked by an even, daily living unto God.

In every case of true conversion the result is the same, a new nature; but that result is produced by a great variety of operations. Some are converted as was Paul, some as was John; some are made to quake under the power of their convictions and in view of the terror of the law; some are so drawn by the cords of love as to feel but little of the one and to see but little of the other. To judge of the truth of conversion by its attending circumstances is to commit a great and practical mistake; and to try a true Christian experience by the same uniform test, is a sure proof of spiritual quackery. The process of reasoning that convinces one is a tissue of sophistry to another; the arguments that induce one to bow at the foot of the cross for mercy are utterly beyond the comprehension of another. Hence the importance of different ministers to suit the varying grades of intelligence; and as different kinds of trees require a different soil and culture to secure their best growth and their best fruit, so different classes of people require a culture suited to their tastes, intelligence, and dispositions, to secure their growth in grace. Hence the forms that refresh some would starve others, and the warm excitement of a Methodist camp-meeting, that is blessed to some, repels others; some are driven to the fold of God by the earthquake, the thunder, the lightning; some are drawn to it by the still, small voice; some are best nourished to a vigorous growth in grace amid the gorgeous forms or high excitements of worship; others by a simple, spiritual worship, quiet as the gently flowing river whose murmurs are never heard, and which, while it fertilized all on its banks, reflects the image of heaven. "The wind bloweth where it listeth, and thou hearest the sound thereof, but canst not tell whence it cometh or whither it goeth; so is every one that is born of the Spirit." "There are differences of administrations, but the same Lord; and there are diversities of operations, but it is the same God who worketh all in all." And who, with even a few years' experience in the ministry, has not found many illustrations of these plain, common-sense principles?

Miss ——— was the child of moral but not religious parents. She was brought up in a community where there were no means of grace save those which were fanatical, and rather repellant than attractive. She was sent away to a boarding-school, and returned to take the first position among the educated and fashionable of her native town. She came some miles to attend on my ministry. I soon perceived that she was deeply interested, and sought an interview with her. Her mind was bright, intelligent, and, save on religious subjects, well instructed. As I unfolded the doctrines of the Gospel, she gave her ready assent to them all. As I placed Christ before her in the fullness of his salvation, she saw at once that he was the end of the law for righteousness to every one that believed on him, and, without hesitation, accepted of him as her Savior. There seemed to be no deep conviction, no conversion, and yet the thing required, faith, was there, and in its most sweet and lovely exercises. Without any noise, or any special attention, or any solicitation, she became a member of the Church. As a lamb enters the flock, she sought a place among the people of God; and for a quarter of a century she has lived to be a blessing to the Church and to adorn her profession. She could tell you of the love of God shed abroad in her heart; but of the deep convictions of Christian in the Pilgrim's Progress, and of the terrible doubts and fears of Payson, she had no experience. And a merchant, known and honored for many years in all the ways of mercantile, Christian, and philanthropic life, in the city of New York, and whose path, from the day he professed Christ until that of his death, was "as the shining light," was often heard to say that he knew nothing of conviction, a part of the usual process by which sinners are usually led to the knowledge of the truth as it is in Jesus. "There are diversities of operations, but it is the same spirit."

Mrs. L—— was brought up a papist, and, of course, in utter ignorance of the Bible and its religion. Good sense, and some travel, and much intercourse with people of other faith, had so weakened the influence of her bad education over her, that she could occasionally worship within Protestant churches. She became an occasional, and then a frequent attendant on my ministry. On her solicitation, I made her a visit. She gave me an intelligent narrative of her life and of her then state of mind. She had been reading the Bible, and was much in prayer. As she needed the sincere milk of the word, I explained to her, in a manner the most simple, the leading doctrines of the Gospel. When I concluded, she said, with emphasis, "This is just what I wanted to know; this is just the religion I need." I prayed with her, and before I retired she was rejoicing in the Lord, and joying in the God of her salvation. Her subsequent life proved it to be a work of the Spirit.

Miss ——— was brought up in a circle of fashion, where the form of religion was respected, but its spirituality and power totally disregarded. Her powers of mind and her education were in advance of those around her, among whom, by her rapid perception, and keen wit, and generous bearing, she was an oracle. She became an attendant on my ministry, and soon deeply anxious about her soul. Her convictions were of the deepest character. Fearing and quaking, she stood, for weeks together, in the very presence of Sinai convulsed with tempests; and when the voice of Mercy seemed to rise above the tempest, and its melting accents fell upon her ear, she would scarcely hear it. Her unbelief was strong beyond expression. She quarreled with every doctrine and every duty; and nothing was believed or done only as the convicting Spirit subdued her obstinate unbelief. Finally the citadel of the heart was captured, and without another struggle she yielded to the commands of her Master. Her promptness to obey was now as great as was her perverse obstinacy; and, thinking that she could almost see the steps by which she ascended from the horrible pit and the miry clay, she yielded herself a living sacrifice to Christ, feeling it to be a reasonable service; and a useful, consistent, and devoted life for many years proved that the change wrought upon her was the work of God. "There are different operations, but it is the same Spirit."

The Lord, with whom alone is the power to renew the heart, has no one mould into which to cast all hearts. He uses very different means to take away the heart of stone and to give a heart of flesh; and he uses very different means for the cultivation of the graces of his people. He leads his people by ways that they knew not onward to the fullness of the stature of perfect men in Christ Jesus. But while the means are diverse, the result is always the same, faith—faith bearing good fruit; and the means are of trifling importance compared with the result; and when convinced that the heart is changed, I care nothing about the means; and, while there is a wide difference in the green pastures, yet I will rejoice over all that are feeding in any of them.

Let us beware of confining the Spirit, in the putting forth of its divine influence, to any of our rules, or forms, or Church notions. Let us beware of condemning all in the way of profession or experience which is not in accordance with our standards. Where we see true faith bearing good fruit, let us cultivate brotherly kindness, knowing that "there are different operations, but it is the same Spirit." Luther and Calvin differed; so did Wesley and Whitfield; and so did Dr. Mason and Bishop Hobart; but they are now rejoicing in heaven; and so will all the children of faith when their work is ended. I would not advise the laying aside of our peculiarities, but I would strongly advise to regard them as entirely secondary to faith in Christ, for this is the saving grace.

I have no disposition to cut off any who believe in Christ from the kingdom of heaven; but of all men, those most deserve this excision who exclude all from the grace and favor of God but themselves. All such are wholesale schismatics.

THE SORROWFUL SERMON.

It was the day of my weekly lecture, and but a few months after my second settlement as a pastor. I spent the morning in my study in preparation for the Sabbath, but there was no excitement of thought or feeling on my mind or heart. The most important truths had lost all their connection, vitality, and freshness, and seemed to lie before me like a bundle of dry sticks; and to produce a thought seemed as impossible as to draw water from an empty well with a bucket without a bottom; and the morning was spent in the vain effort to arrange some ideas on a selected text worthy of being placed on paper. Mind and heart seemed as barren as the sands of the desert.

The afternoon was given to preparation for the evening lecture, but there was no lifting up of that "blackness of darkness." It became denser with the approach of evening. The Bible was turned over from cover to cover, but not a text could be found from which a sentiment or meaning could be drawn adapted to the occasion or to the audience which usually met in the lecture-room. The very avenues to the throne of grace seemed barred up against all access to God, so that I could truly say, in the language of Job, "Behold, I go forward, but he is not there; and backward, but I can not perceive him; on the left hand, where he doth work, but I can not behold him; he hideth himself on the right hand, that I can not see him." Of all the days of my life, that was the day in which I could say most emphatically, as to spiritual things, that "a horror of great darkness" had fallen upon me. The sun, moon, and stars had all gone out in my spiritual sky.

The bell rang for the evening service, and its first notes fell upon my ear as a death-knell. Slowly and sorrowfully I went to that meeting with my people, my mind a perfect blank, and without a text or subject on which to discourse to them. It was a charming night in October, when the moon was shining brightly, and, to my regret, I found the lecture-room unusually full. I resolved to change the service into a meeting for prayer, and commenced it with the hymn,

"How long wilt thou conceal thy face?
My God, how long delay?
When shall I feel those heavenly rays
That chase my fears away?"

I called upon an aged elder to pray, who prayed with remarkable devotion of thought and with great unction. Because in consonance with my feelings, I read the 42d Psalm, and my heart could truly respond to the sentiment of the Psalmist: "O my God, my soul is cast down within me . . . all thy waves and thy billows are gone over me." But I was yet without a text or subject on which to address the people. I called upon another elder to pray, who in his supplications entered fully into the spirit of the psalm; and while he confessed and bewailed our spiritual desertion, most fervently implored that the Lord would again "give us a little reviving in our bondage." It was during this prayer, and, indeed, by the prayer itself, that the topic of "declension in religion" was suggested as a theme for remark. Drawing largely on the existing feelings of my own mind and heart, without a text, and without knowing what I was going to say when I commenced, I entered upon the topic, and said something on the causes, marks, and remedy of spiritual declension. The following language of Cecil was brought seasonably to my remembrance, and was quoted for substance: "A Christian may decline far in religion without being suspected; he may maintain appearances. Every thing to others seems to go on well. He suspects himself; for it requires great labor to maintain appearances, especially in a minister. Discerning hearers will, however, often detect such declensions. He talks over his old matters. He says his things, but in a cold and unfeeling manner. He is sound, indeed, in doctrine; perhaps more sound than before, for there is a great tendency to soundness of doctrine when appearances are to be kept up in a declining state of the heart. Where a man has real grace, it may be a part of a dispensation toward him to permit him to decline. He walked carelessly; he was left to decline, that he might be brought to feel his need of vigilance. If he is indulging a besetting sin, it may please God to expose him, that he may hang down his head as long as he lives. But this is pulling down in order to build up."*

* Cecil's Remains, p. 182.

As I proceeded, the subject seemed to open up before me, but I felt that I condemned myself at every sentence; and at the conclusion of a disconnected, fragmentary address, I called upon another person to conclude the meeting with prayer. On the conclusion of the services, I returned to my study dejected, and oppressed with a sense of my being forsaken of God, and grieved that I had ever assumed the responsibilities of the ministry.

On the afternoon of the next day, an intelligent and pious female called to see me. She alluded to the service of the previous evening as being one of the most solemn she had recently attended. I heard her with silence, and made no response. One of the men who prayed soon afterward called; he made the same remark. The solemnity of that evening's lecture was a topic of conversation for some days with those who were present. The prayer-meetings were soon more fully attended. There were searchings of heart among the people. Our public and social services increased in attendance and solemnity. The praying and the anxious ones, as they invariably do, multiplied simultaneously; and thus opened the first revival, in my second settlement, under my ministry, and which continued for upward of a year, gently distilling its blessed influences, multiplying the followers of Christ and their graces. Some of its subjects are now faithful and useful ministers of the Gospel. Never did I more fully realize the truth of the proverb, that "the darkest hour is just before the light," or of the saying of the Psalmist, "He that goeth forth and weepeth, bearing precious seed, shall doubtless come again with rejoicing bearing his sheaves with him."

This dark and yet joyful incident is here noted, not because of its peculiarity, as there are but few ministers who have not a similar experience, but for the purpose of bringing out a few of the principles of which it is an illustration.

The hiding of God's countenance is not always desertion. We are backward in duty, we are negligent in its performance, we are self-confident, we are worldly. We keep not the Lord always before us. For these, or for some other sins, and for their reproof, God may withdraw the light of his countenance; and then we walk in darkness, as does the traveler at midnight, when the sun, moon, and stars have withdrawn their shining; and on all such occasions the people of the Lord should inquire, "Why art thou cast down, O my soul, and why art thou disquieted within me? Hope thou in God; for I shall yet praise him who is the health of my countenance and my God." On due inquiry, we will find that no new thing has happened to us—that a part of God's dispensations to his people is to show them their weakness by leaving them to themselves, and to demonstrate their constant need of him by leaving them occasionally to tread the weary ways of life by the light of the sparks of their own kindling. And we should be careful how we violate the principle thus taught and sung,

"Judge not the Lord by feeble sense,
But trust him for his grace;
Behind a frowning providence
He hides a smiling face."

May it not be that ministers preach too little from their own varying experience? If truly good men, their experience, in its main outlines, is that of all the Lord's people. Preachingon doctrines strengthens and enlightens—on duties, stimulates to action: exhortatory preaching may quicken the footsteps of the indolent; but when they preach from their own deep, heartfelt experience, and whether the string they touch gives forth notes of joy or sorrow, they find notes responsive in the hearts of many hearers. The seat of religion is the heart; and when they preach from an experience of the power of the grace of God in their own hearts, they are more likely to reach the hearts of their hearers.

May it not be that the unvarying sameness which has obtained in our stated public and social services, detracts from their power and usefulness? How often do ministers hear least about the preparations on which they have bestowed most labor; and most about the warm, heartfelt addresses made to meet an emergency, and without any previous preparation! I have often observed that a warm, blundering man does far more for the world than a stately, correct, and frigid one. When we get into the habit of inquiring on all occasions, great and small, as to proprieties and expediencies, life is too often spent to little purpose. Nature craves for variety; and eccleseology would reduce every thing to an unvarying form in public and social worship. Such forms of worship are as unnatural as they are injurious. Sermons occasionally without texts—sermons sometimes without music or prayers—and prayers and singing sometimes without sermons, would break in upon the monotony which has almost universally obtained, and would, at least, so far lead to awaken attention to the truth of God. We would not imitate the example of the eccentric preacher, who, on seeing his hearers sleeping around him, cried out "Fire! Fire!" and when the aroused people asked "where? where?" replied, "for sleeping souls in hell;" but we would recommend a studied effort to introduce variety into all the services of God, for the sake of our common humanity, and because of the good which may result. It is said of the excellent Cecil, that he often omitted family prayer, for the purpose of breaking in upon what might otherwise be regarded as a very unmeaning and heartless form.

I have never forgotten the impressions, and hope never to forget the lessons, taught me by that sorrowful sermon.

BEASTS AT EPHESUS.

The difficulties amid which the Gospel of salvation has been preached have been substantially the same in every age. Pagan and papal Rome have shed the blood of the martyrs, and so have papal and Protestant Britain. The carnal heart is enmity toward God, and the cross of Christ is yet to the Jews a stumbling block, and to the Greeks foolishness; and the opposition of the unchanged heart to the Gospel is the same now as when the persecuting Cæsars reigned on the Tiber—as when Paul fought with beasts at Ephesus—modified in its actings only by humane laws, advancing civilization, and the general prevalence of the spirit of Christianity.

Of this general truth, the history of the labors of many of the domestic missionaries of every evangelical Church in the United States would furnish abundant illustration. These laborious and excellent men endure many privations, and have many severe conflicts with those who oppose themselves. Out, as they mainly are, on the selvages of society, and among those least morally instructed, whose passions are strong, and whose errors are often as bold as they are absurd and wicked, they often require great courage and nerve to stem the open opposition often made to them because they preach the doctrine of repentance toward God and faith in our Lord Jesus Christ.

I commenced my ministry when "protracted meetings" were popular, and when the evangelists, by whom they were conducted on the highest key of excitement, were regarded as "the angels of the churches." And although connected with a class of ministers who never favored "the revival evangelists," and who opposed the "new measures" of which "anxious seats" were the representative, yet we yielded so far to the popular feeling of the Church as to hold protracted meetings, which were conducted by ourselves without foreign aid and without new measures. For the purpose of illustrating the power of the Gospel, and the kind of opposition with which it has not unfrequently to meet, I will give a brief narrative of one of those meetings.

T—— was a town of some importance in Northern Pennsylvania. Its first settlers were chiefly from New England—men of enterprise and shrewdness, but without religion. It became the county town, and had its court-house, and jail, and taverns, but no church of any kind. Universalism and infidelity were there, and united their forces to oppose every effort to introduce the Gospel into the community. The only preaching-place was the Court-house, and, as every body had a right to go there, many thought they had a right to treat the minister when preaching as they were accustomed to treat the politician when making a political harangue, and especially to treat with rudeness what did not agree with their prejudices; and this right was often queerly exercised by interrupting a preacher, by putting questions to him in the midst of his sermon, by persons getting up and leaving the room, and, as they retired, pronouncing some truth declared to be a d—d lie. Nor were these things done simply by the rabble; they were practiced and countenanced by men of intelligence and position. These things, and the morals which they cherished, obtained for the town, at a distance, the name of "Satan's Seat," and caused many a good minister to fear to preach the Gospel there, lest he should be attacked and insulted by these emissaries of Satan, these beasts at Ephesus.

It was in this town that a neighboring pastor of excellent and prudent character resolved to hold a protracted meeting, and to invite some of his brethren to his assistance. I was of the number invited. Our only preaching-place was the Court-house, which was duly secured for our purposes, and the meeting was generally advertised for weeks previous; and expectation was on tiptoe as to our meeting, its disturbance, and its results. Threats were made beforehand, and by men who lacked neither the energy nor the impudence to carry out their most wicked purposes. To be forewarned is to be forearmed, and we went to the Court-house prepared for an attack, but in what way it was to come we knew not.

It was in the evening. The room was crowded. It was with difficulty that the ministers could make their way to the seat occupied by the judges when the court was in session. As the preliminary services were being performed, I strove to read, as I could, the crowd around me. Just beneath me was the green table around which the lawyers sat when at court, and around the niche in that table sat a few individuals, whose object in coming to the meeting could not be mistaken. Their whisperings, winkings, and noddings satisfied me as to the quarter from which difficulty might be expected; and I plainly saw that they had their sympathizers and opposers in the crowd. Conspicuous among them was a Campbellite Baptist preacher, of low character, and a lawyer of the place, who was said to be like his father, and a little more so; the character of that father was a hybrid, such as we might expect to be produced by now pettifogging, and now acting as Universalist exhorter. These two men were the leaders.

As I arose to preach, I paused a moment to take a close survey of these men. They were just beneath me. As their gaze met mine, they dropped their heads. I saw in a moment they were only braggarts that could be soon driven to the wall. Save the rustling of their paper, on which they were making notes, every thing was quiet to the close of the service. The moment the benediction was pronounced, the Campbellite Baptist sprung to his feet and screamed out, "I wish to know whether I may ask the preacher a few questions?" The crowd, which commenced moving, was brought to a dead pause, and waited in breathless silence for a reply. Some felt that the fight was now fairly opened. After a brief pause, I replied as follows: "We have come here to preach the Gospel for a few days to those who may choose to come and hear us. One of our principles is to disturb nobody in their religious worship; and another is, to allow nobody to disturb us. There is a law to protect us from disturbance, and we shall see that that law is enforced." Then turning to the man who asked the question, I said to him, "You are either an honest or dishonest inquirer: if an honest one, you may come to my lodgings, and I will answer, as far as I am able, any of your questions; if a dishonest one, as I fear you are, I wish to have nothing to do with you, here or there." He could make no reply, and the crowd dispersed applauding the positions taken, but yet feeling that the end of the chapter was not yet.

As the meetings progressed, a deep solemnity was soon observable. As the gainsayers were regularly at their post, there was a constant crowd in attendance, in expectation, daily, of some conflict. In the evening they came in great numbers from the surrounding country, and long before the hour of service the Court-house was crowded to its utmost capacity. At the conclusion of a deeply solemn service one evening, we invited the serious to retire to a room in the building for religious conversation. As we entered the room, to our astonishment, we found there a large number of persons deeply anxious, among whom were some prominent citizens; and conspicuous among them was the Campbellite preacher and his friend the lawyer. I saw, at a glance, that accounts must be first settled with these before we could proceed; and, approaching the preacher, I asked him sternly, "What, sir, is your object in coming here?" "I want you," he replied, "to give right instruction to these anxious sinners; and for this purpose I wish you to read this chapter." And, suiting the action to the word, he put a small Bible, opened, into my hands. Amazed at his cool impertinence, I returned the Bible, saying, "When, sir, we need your counsel and aid, we will send for you; and as we did not invite you here, you will leave the room." And as it was now my turn to suit the action to the word, I gently laid my hand upon his shoulder and pointed to the door, and, to my surprise, he went quietly away. Wickedness is always cowardly.

Having gotten rid of one customer, I then approached the lawyer, who had obviously more daring about him than the ignorant, unmannerly preacher. "And what, sir," said I, "is your object in coming here?" Stretching himself to his highest altitude, and in a semi-comic way, designed to produce merriment in that anxious-room, he replied, "You have said something in your sermon to-night about the devil, and I thought I would come and ask you who the devil is." Feeling that it was one of those occasions which would justify the answering of a fool according to his folly, I replied, "You are the first man I have met, for some time, that did not know who his father was." The question and answer were heard by all in the room. I then said to him, as to his companion in wickedness, "As we did not invite you here, sir, you will leave the room." Soon the comic was changed to the tragic aspect, and he declared, "I will not leave the room; this house is a county house, and is free and open to us all; I have as good a right to be here as you have." It so happened that among the inquirers was an aged, athletic man, a prominent citizen, and an associate judge of the county; and I said to him, "Judge, will you see that Mr. —— leaves the room." He rose at once, and said to him, "Mr. ——, you will leave the room, sir." There was no alternative but to leave, and he went out enraged; and he went down the stairs swearing that he would shoot me, as sure as he was a living man. The door was then closed; we proceeded with our service, and a more deeply-impressed company of anxious inquirers, asking what they should do to be saved, I never saw.

The services of the evening ended. There was a deep excitement upon many minds as to what the enraged lawyer would do. Six or eight men accompanied me, or kept near me, on my way to my lodgings. They feared his violence; but when I knew their object, I told them there was nothing to fear, as I soon saw the man was only a braggart. The question he asked up stairs, and the reply to it, soon got into circulation. The interview was all over town the next day, and every where the old man was hailed as "the old devil," and the enraged lawyer as "the young devil." There were some who affirmed that rarely could the epithets be more appropriately applied.

That was the end of the lawyer as far as our services were concerned; but the preacher regularly attended them. He lodged at the public house, and it was whispered that he did not always drink cold water. After a solemn meeting, in which the preacher strongly presented the idea that morality, however spotless in the view of man, could not save a sinner, in making his way through the crowd, he said, "Let me go where morality is more respected than here!" I saw the hit would have its effect upon some minds, and in a low, but yet audible tone, said, "The gentleman wants to get to the tavern." He got out, and that was the end of him.

The services subsequently proceeded without any disturbance of any kind. The solemnity increased from day to day. The Gospel was joyfully received by many in that town and in the surrounding country. A church was organized, of which those hopefully converted at that protracted meeting were the main elements. A church was soon erected. That ungodly clique was broken up, and its chief members converted into laughing-stocks. Twenty-five years have nearly passed away since that meeting, through which its influence for good has been felt on all the interests of society. That once wicked town is now the seat of several churches, and of, at least, one moral and educational institution, which is destined to shed its light on the surrounding country, and for ages to come.

What has become of that Campbellite preacher, I know not. He was, beyond doubt, a bad man. If yet living, may the Lord convert him. The lawyer to get rid of the sobriquet, "the young devil," went to parts unknown, and thus happily relieved the community from his evil example. One of the beloved men who preached on that occasion has gone up to his reward, while three yet survive who were engaged in this conflict with beasts at Ephesus.

The malignity of these men was overruled for good.

They overshot the line of even allowed opposition there, and disgusted many. They made show of fight, and attracted multitudes to witness the affray. Thus they multiplied the hearers of the Gospel and the trophies of the cross. The Lord often makes the use of wicked men that sportsmen do of their dogs—the dogs start the birds, and then the sportsmen shoot them; so that beasts at Ephesus have their place in the economy of redemption. What they mean for evil the Lord overrules for good.

DRIFT-WOOD.

The first years of my ministry were spent on the banks of the Susquehanna, and in one of the most beautiful valleys upon earth. It has been my lot to wander upon foreign shores. I have gazed upon Italian skies and scenes; I have wandered over the mountains and vales of Switzerland; I have traversed the Rhine, the Rhone, the Clyde; I have gazed upon most of the beautiful scenery of Britain, and yet I turn to Wyoming as unsurpassed in quiet beauty by any vale that I have ever seen.

> "A valley from the river shore withdrawn;
> * * * * *
> So sweet a spot of earth, you might, I ween,
> Have guessed some congregation of the elves,
> To sport by summer moon, had shaped it for themselves."

The river by which it is divided, enriched, and greatly beautified, is subject to freshets. This is caused, in the spring, by the sudden melting of the snow in the mountain ranges in which it has its rise, and at other seasons of the year by heavy rains. When swollen, as I have often seen it, it rushes on with fearful rapidity and violence, sweeping to destruction every thing that lies in its way; and when thus swollen, often have I stood on its banks, and gazed with trembling on the terrific current sweeping away houses, mills, trees torn from its banks, and rotten wood of all kinds and sizes, and whirling them in every direction as if they were but corks.

These freshets were occasions of some importance to that class of people, too large in every community, who live by their wits. These, taking their position on the bank of the river with fit implements, were laborious in their efforts to fish from the turbulent current the floating timbers. They were often successful, and in a few days would pile on the shore drift-wood enough to supply them with fuel for a few months. It was quite amusing to witness the scenes which often occurred. When a large timber was seen in the distance, each was anxious to be its captor. One would harpoon it, and when shouting out, "I have it," the force of the current would sweep it away; and thus many would successively harpoon it, but yet it would escape from them all. The size of the log and the force of the current gave it a momentum that no arm could resist. Great exertion was often made to bring a drift to the shore; but when caught, it was found worthless, and was cast back again into the foaming waters. At a sharp turn in the river much lumber was driven on shore, and to that spot many would rush, hoping there to catch a fine log, but it would shoot round the corner and disappoint them all. Some lumber would float into an eddy, or would get entangled among the trees on the low bottoms, or would be caught by a pier, where it was considered secure; but, on a sudden, the power of the current would drive it into the middle of the river, and down it would go, disappointing all hopes. When the freshet rapidly subsided, much lumber was left upon the dry land, there to remain until another should come and carry it farther down toward the ocean. It was not even picked up as fuel for the fire. One thing was very observable, that the drift-wood was but rarely fitted to be wrought into a building, or to be used for any ornamental purpose. It was usually gathered into heaps, and when sufficiently dry, to be burned.

And all this is but the type of what is constantly occurring in society around us. Are there not freshets in society as upon our great rivers; excitements, political, moral, and religious, which work great changes, which reveal men of principle, which tear up and send adrift those not rooted and grounded in the truth? In what community or in what calling are not persons to be found whose only fit emblem is drift-wood?

I had a college-mate of many good qualities. He was fluent, rapid in his conceptions, a professor of religion, but vain and ambitious. He was a candidate for the ministry. But there were indications that his vanity was stronger than his principles, and that to feed the one he would sacrifice the other. The freshet came in our junior year, when, on the giving out of the appointments which indicated the standing of the students as scholars, he failed to obtain any. He expected one of the highest; he got none. His pride was mortified beyond endurance—he left college—he gave up the ministry—he made shipwreck of faith—he went out upon the sweeping tide of politics, where, no doubt, unless radically changed, his principles are yet the weaker, and his vanity the stronger power. Such persons can never be any thing but drift-wood.

I had a theological class-mate of very good qualities. He was good-looking—he dressed well—he wrote poetry—he flattered, and was flattered by, the ladies. He knew more about Tom Moore than Turretin; he read Greek less than Goëthe; he preferred Walter to Thomas Scott, and could quote Byron at least as well as the Bible. Vanity was his besetting sin. He got license to preach, but could get no settlement. Thinking that the people of the Church of his fathers were too dull to appreciate his shining qualities, he passed over to another. To be in keeping with his high flights, he became High-Church, and whither the freshet has carried him I know not. He has written a book, as I learn, on "The Succession," of which he knows as much as about the precession of the equinoxes, and which has only served to prove that he was, or is, drift-wood.

I had yet another fellow-student. He was young, ruddy, and prepossessing. Although yet in his teens, he was deeply imbued with the spirit of New Measures, then on the high tide of successful experiment. He denounced his teachers as pharisees and fogies. While yet a student, he practiced his new notions in a small way. Finding but little encouragement for his novelties, he changed his latitude for more congenial climes. He entered the ministry a New-measure man, greatly exciting the hopes of their friends. He went abroad, and became enamored of the old, petrified measures of the Old World, and on his return deserted his former friends. Now, excitements were only injurious, and Church power and set forms were every thing. This was a change from the equator to the poles. For a while he linked himself with the straitest sects of the Church of his fathers, but that did not long suffice. He was on the bosom of the swollen river, and could not stop. At a bound he became a Puseyite, and, whether for funds or to make friends, wrote one of the most disgraceful and truthless books known to theological controversy in modern days. The book by "One of Three Hundred" proves, at least, that its author was of the drift-wood species. He had no root in himself; he was the prey of every current; and if he had remained a little longer, another swell of the freshet would have swept him from his Oxford eddy, and would have left him deep in the mud of the Tiber, praying to the Virgin to take him out and clean him off.

Another specimen of the same genus. He was bold, bluff, and self-confident. When a student he went to three colleges, and claimed credit for it! He went, at least, to three seminaries, to get the good of each. He was educated a Presbyterian, ordained a Congregationalist, became, I believe, a Methodist, then a Baptist; but what he now is, I know not, nor does he know himself. Each thought they had him, but he escaped from them all. The harpoon entered the log in a soft place, where it could not hold. What has become of him I know not; but when next drawn to the shore, he may be cast back again into the current as too worthless to repay the trouble of fishing him out.

There are exceptions to all general rules. In the course of his studies, a young man may see reasons sufficient to leave the Church of his early education for some other. No man is bound to the faith of his fathers, because, if so, the Jew must remain a Jew, the pagan a pagan, the papist a papist, forever. No young man is to be censured for departing from the faith of his fathers, if he does so for reasons, and wisely. But when men have formed their opinions, and preached them for years, and then change them, it is an evidence of a restless, disordered state of mind. One or two attacks of any disease renders the system liable to its return; and one or two changes in opinions is liable to convert the individual into a changeling, and to send him out upon the stream of life as drift-wood.

And how many there are connected, as private members, with the churches whose only fit emblem is drift-wood. They go here and there as prejudice, or passion, or fashion, or some disappointment may sway them. I knew an elder twice censured in a Presbytery, who, in revenge, became a most violent High-Churchman, and had all his children rebaptized for conscience' sake! Mr. —— and family were from England; according to their own showing, they left the husks of the Establishment for the simple truth of the Independents. They then attached themselves to the ministry of some supralapsarian shoemaker. They came to this country, but for a long time could find no suitable successor to the shoemaker. As I was considered as coming nearest to him, they placed themselves under my ministry. For a time they would have plucked out their eyes and given them to me; but the Millerite fever became epidemic, and they caught it badly. The fanatics of that threadbare nonsense became their favorites. I no longer preached the Gospel, because I did not preach up the destruction of the world about Easter, and advise the faithful to commence cutting their ascension robes. They were swept out as drift-wood upon the bosom of the freshet, but where it has carried them is hardly worth the inquiry.

And persons of whom drift-wood is the true emblem are to be found in every community, and attached to all congregations. They are as numerous as those who are ungoverned by fixed principles. There are those in the ministry who can pass from this body to that, from this school to that, with all ease. These regard themselves, and would be regarded by others, as moderate and catholic. But there is another explanation for all this; their own lines of opinion are drawn with invisible ink, and can be shifted to suit circumstances; they have no root in themselves. There are those in the churches upon whom you can make no calculation. The next freshet may carry them into some new connection, or work a change in their entire views and feelings. I look around me, and see persons who have been connected with three churches in less than three years. I see others who have passed from one denomination to another because their minister did not like secret societies, or preach up, to the point of scalding heat, the efficacy of some plans of social reform. And there are but few churches in the land where the freshets to which human opinions and society are ever liable have not deposited some of this drift-wood, where it will remain until the rise of another freshet, when it will be again swept out and whirled we know not whither. When the tree is torn up by the roots and swept into the current, there is no telling where it will stop; and if brought to shore, it will be difficult to replant it. It will not pay for the labor. Dr. Priestley was once a high Calvinist, then a low one; then an Armenian; then a high Arian, then a low one; then a Unitarian; then a Humanitarian; and he was once heard to say, "If God spares me a few years more, I know not what I shall be before I die." When a stone is started on the brow of the mountain, it is hard to stop it until it reaches the bottom.

Many make a great noise when a minister, or persons in high position, pass over to them. But they have caught only drift-wood. How long they can keep them is uncertain; and to what use they can put them is often a question.

There are those who are steadfast, immovable, always abounding in the works of the Lord, and those who are ever learning and never coming to the knowledge of the truth. The first are as the cedars in Lebanon, that bear fruit even to old age, and that are fit to be converted to the most useful purposes in the house of the Lord; the second are but drift-wood, scarcely fit to feed the fires that warm it.

A MOTHER IN ISRAEL.

It will never be known, until the day of final revealing, how much the Church of God and the world owes to the prayers, the teachings, the quiet, home influence of Christian woman. What pastor is there that does not acknowledge her powerful influence for good in every department of usefulness? And were it possible to subtract from the entire influence of the Church all that is contributed to it by Christian woman, it would be weakened to a degree of which we can scarcely form a conception. If Spartan mothers made heroes by devoting their sons on the altar of their country to its service, Christian mothers have made martyrs, and missionaries, and ministers, and incorruptible patriots, and true citizens, by devoting them on the altars of the Church to their God. A woman of sense, of strong principles, and of consistent, firm piety, will make her impression upon her children. She will give form and direction to their tastes before they know it; and in the school-room, among their playmates, and even in the highest moods of frolic and fun, they will testify to her influence by their superior conduct. The good Josiah was the son of Amon, a monster in wickedness, and the grandson of Manasseh, under whose superlatively wicked reign the Hebrews sunk to a lower depth in departure from God than did the Canaanites before them; but his mother was a pious woman. And when the sacred historian would tell us that "Josiah was eight years old when he began to reign," and that "he did that which was right in the sight of the Lord, and walked in all the ways of David his father, and turned not aside to the right hand or to the left," he would also inform us, as if to account for the whole, that "his mother's name was Jedidah." As a mother in Israel, Jedidah devoted her infant son to God; she prayed around his cradle; she instilled divine principles into his youthful mind; she taught him to fear God, and to fear nothing else; and when Amon, her husband, fell by the murderous daggers of his own servants, in his own house, and when the people made the princely boy king in his place, it is said, boy as he was, that "he did that which was right in the sight of the Lord." "While he was yet young, he began to seek after the God of David his father; and in his twelfth year he began to purge Judah and Jerusalem from the high places." After reigning thirty-one years, he was slain in battle in the valley of Megiddo; "and all Judah and Jerusalem mourned for Josiah." And his pious youth, and his prosperous reign, and the holy influence that went out from his throne over all his kingdom, may be traced, under God, to the piety and precepts of his mother. "His mother's name was Jedidah."

Such a mother in Israel it has been my great privilege to know. She was among the kindest friends and wisest counselors of my early ministry; and although years have passed away since her departure for the

Church triumphant, the savor of her name and memory is as sweet ointment poured forth.

She was the daughter of a New England clergyman, and was descended from a Puritan family, many of whose members rose to distinction in the Church and in the state. She became, while yet young, the wife of a merchant in her native state, who for years was engaged in prosperous business. By some of the reverses of trade, his property was suddenly swept away like stubble before the conflagration, and he was reduced to poverty. The effect upon him was unhappy through life; his spirits were broken, and he fell into bad habits. They removed from New England, and on my first settlement I found them connected with my congregation, far advanced in life, and with a most interesting family of children. Although not in affluent circumstances, yet were they such a family as immediately attracted attention, and commanded respect beyond what wealth could purchase.

I first saw that good old lady in her seat in the Church. She was there when I entered it. She wore her glasses, and through the service appeared remarkably devout; and as if for the purpose of reading me through and through, she looked over them, and through them, as best answered her purpose. Such was the impression she made upon me, that I made inquiry as to who she was before I left the Church.

On my first visit to her she was reserved, and apparently depressed. My predecessor in the ministry was dismissed after a protracted strife, which left many bitter feelings. She adhered to him to the last; and she seemed to regret that, with so little experience, I should launch my frail bark amid waters so troubled. She looked on my youth—she remembered past conflicts—and she was troubled. And all this she most kindly though timidly intimated. She was the least forward, for a woman of her strong sense, that I ever knew.

Her former pastor was afflicted with a natural hesitancy in speaking, which was considerably increased by an attack of paralysis; and his enemies plead this as one among the many reasons for which they urged his removal. But, with a remarkable dexterity, she converted it into an argument for his remaining. "We hear the Gospel," she would say, "with too little thoughtfulness and application. One truth is uttered after another, and before we can weigh one, another is on the top of it, and another on the top of that; and thus the Gospel runs through our minds like water through a glass tube: none of it sticks; and when we come home, we remember nothing that we have heard. Now I like these long pauses of Mr. G——, because they give me time to pack away what he says." On first hearing this sentiment from her own lips, I immediately formed my estimate of her, which I had never reason to change, save on the side of a higher admiration of her character.

Although, when interested, her conversational powers were very fine and remarkably suggestive, yet she was habitually reserved. Her voice was never heard in the street, nor in the social gathering, save in its low tones. She was candid in her opinions, deliberate in the formation of them, and cautious in their utterance; but when formed, she never yielded them save for a reason, and always changed them for a good reason. Hence she was an oracle to many, and her opinions were the law of her household. So extended was her knowledge of Christian doctrine and experience, that she could resolve perplexity as to either with remarkable skill; and her advice was constantly sought by the serious, the inquiring, and the desponding.

The excuse she made for her former pastor revealed her manner of hearing the Gospel. She always prepared for the house of God—was always there when able to go—and heard with devotion and application. She would let the commonplaces go; but she would seize with avidity upon important truths, and would "pack them away," to be brought out on future occasions for use. She cared far less about the manner than the matter; and when persons would be depreciating ministers because of their dullness or want of elegance, she would quote some sentiments to which they had given utterance, and would say, "Until I do all they have taught me, I have no fault to find."

Her devotional spirit was of a marked character. She was not an ascetic—she had no ritual hours—she was no believer in the virtue of forms; and while I know nothing about her closet hours, I never found her otherwise than in a devotional frame. God, to her, was every where and in every thing; and she sought to do all she did as under his eye and to the glory of his name. Her devotion was not confined to the Sabbath nor to set occasions: it was habitual. While she had her alternations of depression and joyfulness, the omnipresence of God was often a theme of remark, and she could say,

> "Within thy circling power I stand,
> On every side I find thy hand;
> Awake, asleep, at home, abroad,
> I am surrounded still with God."

And a constant sense of his presence acted as fuel to feed the fires of her devotion. Often have I seen her remaining in the church until all had left it, as if praying that the services might be blessed of the Lord, and then quietly walking alone to her house, as if "packing away" and applying the truth that had been preached.

Her principles never yielded to her prejudices or affections. They were her rule and law. A remarkable instance and illustration of this she gave in the case of her youngest child. She called him by the name of her New England pastor, to whom she was remarkably attached, and to whom also she owed a debt of gratitude for many kind favors. He became an avowed Unitarian; and the moment she was convinced that her friend and benefactor had denied the divinity of her Lord and Master, her sense of gratitude and her strong affection yielded to her principles. She changed the name of her son; and he yet lives, bearing and honoring the name of one of Old England's noblest judges, instead of that of an apostate from the truth as it is in Jesus.

Her faith in God was strong, and but rarely wavering. It was to her the substance of things hoped for, and the evidence of things not seen. During a protracted service, in which those eloquent and sainted men, Winchester and Dr. John Breckenridge, assisted, she was a constant and devout attendant; and when a service would conclude without any apparent results, she would ask, "Wherefore this waste? wherefore this waste?" She was looking for the descent of the Spirit upon every service, and expressed her disappointment when her anxious prayers were not answered. But they were answered, and in a way that will be felt in that community and for ages to come. She has already commenced the undying song with some who were then born again, and with some who preceded her from her own household.

The salvation of her husband was with her a daily solicitude. His habits were bad; and although amiable, he had grown gray and decrepit in the ways of impenitence. There was every thing in his case to discourage hope; yet her hope in reference to him never wavered. He died of protracted disease, and gave to her, to his children, and to all who visited him, as good an evidence as such cases usually afford, that he died in the Lord. Her remarkable faith in reference to him, and its protracted exercise among difficulties, make his a far more hopeful case than death-bed repentances usually are. I have no doubt but that the soul of her husband is now a shining star in the crown of her rejoicing.

But it was especially upon the minds and hearts ot her children that she left the deepest impression of her character. They resembled her physically. Her ways of thinking, her very tones of voice, they caught. Her prudent caution—her natural reserve—her adherence to principles, were theirs; and although all of them were not converted until after her death, her faith never wavered as to the conversion of them all. She committed them all to the Lord, and she knew that he would keep that which she had committed unto him. Among the last words she ever uttered were these, in reference to her children: "O Lord, all mine are thine." And every one of her children were brought into the Church, the youngest since her happy death, and most of them yet live, filling and adorning positions of distinguished usefulness. One is an eminent jurist, worthy of the place once occupied by a Marshall. One is a clergyman known in all the Church for his abilities and amiable virtues. One was the lovely wife of a minister, whose sun went down before it reached its noontide. Two are ornaments of the bar and of the medical profession. One died in hope, the wife of an army surgeon, and was buried by the waves of the Mississippi. And two others, in the spheres in which they move, are serving their generation according to the will of God.

That mother is gone; but her influence lives in her children, and will be transmitted to her children's children to the remotest times. Such a life as she led is immortal. She was a mother in Israel, and deserves a place, as do many others, by the side of Jocebed, Hannah, and Jedidah, the mothers of the pious Moses, Samuel, and Josiah.

When such mothers are multiplied in Israel, there

will be more piety in the Church, and more patriotism in the state, and more principle every where. A pious, intelligent mother, living by faith, and bringing up her household for heaven, is the highest style of woman.

THE END.

www.ingramcontent.com/pod-product-compliance
Lightning Source LLC
LaVergne TN
LVHW010226110826
845151LV00004B/1200

* 9 7 8 1 4 2 5 5 2 6 0 1 6 *